PRINT EDITION
The Last Timekeepers and the Arch of Atlantis ©
2012 by Sharon Ledwith
Edited by: Justine Dowsett

Published by Mirror World Publishing in June, 2015

Mirror World Publishing
Windsor, Ontario
www.mirrorworldpublishing.com
info@mirrorworldpublishing.com

ISBN: 978-1-987976-03-8

For Michael. My partner, my pillar, my post.

.

The Last Timekeepers

and the Arch of Atlantis

Sharon Ledwith

Prologue

manda Sault silently studied the words she'd just scrawled: *May 1ˢᵗ, 1214—Games and songs and revelry, act as the cloak of devilry. So that an English legend may give to the poor, we must travel to Nottingham to even the score.*

She frowned. She was the Scribe. She was supposed to understand what this riddle meant, but she didn't have a clue. All she knew was that she, her four annoying classmates, and two offbeat adults were standing in what was left of the lost continent of Atlantis and they were supposed to be the Timekeepers, the legendary time travelers handpicked by destiny to keep Earth's history safe from evil. But no one had told them how they were supposed to do it.

Their problem: no matter what happened—good or bad—they weren't supposed to mess with the past. Period. Dot. End of story. Amanda felt hot liquid build in her throat. Her thumb traced the words of the arcane riddle. Their first Timekeeper mission. Amanda knew this wasn't the end of the story.

This was just the beginning.

1. *Food Fight*

"*H*ey, Locohontas!"

Annoyed, Amanda looked up from composing her newest poem as a slice of pizza splattered against her cheek.

"Food fight, food fight!" chanted a couple of boys at the front of the Snack Program line.

Hot, gooey sauce ran down her face. She hastily stuffed her journal and pen down the bib of her faded jean overalls, flicked away a piece of pepperoni stuck to her cheek, then turned to face the enemy. Her chocolate brown eyes burned into the grade-six boys who had started the food flying. A second slice hit Amanda on her other cheek. It just wasn't her day.

The whole school gym went berserk. The two parent volunteers covered their heads and made a run for the side exit door. The walls echoed with laughter and screams as grade sevens and eights ruled supreme. Pizza collided with cement walls and human targets. The few who did escape had either runny cheese in their hair or splattered sauce all over their clothes. Amanda snatched a slice stuck to the floor and looked for a victim. Her eyes crinkled with delight when she spied Ashley Prigham—the girl who had everything and knew it. Amanda hurled the droopy slice. However, her pitch didn't cooperate; the pizza missed Ashley and sailed into Jordan Jensen's face.

Amanda gulped. "Golden Jock" Jensen was probably the most popular and well-liked boy in the entire school, possibly even in the whole town of White Pines. Her shoulders slumped. *Figures. I might as well stand in a pool of quicksand.*

Suddenly, Amanda's knees buckled as if she were really being sucked into the ground. Treena Mui had hit the floor, and then Amanda, with enough force to knock Amanda down. Treena looked up at Amanda like a helpless baby seal.

Amanda knitted her brows. *What's a rich kid like her doing at the Snack Program?*

"S-S-Sorry, Amanda," Treena stammered. "All that sauce on the floor, I guess."

Standing, Amanda waved her hand. "Forget it, Treena."

Treena grunted as she got to her feet, her plump belly jiggling with every move. She started to slip again.

Amanda grabbed Treena's elbow and held her up. White Pines Elementary School's drama club queen wouldn't break a leg on her watch! Treena's dream was to attend the premiere of her first movie within ten years' time. Amanda envisioned some campy teen musical, and then bit her lower lip. At least Treena had a dream. She didn't have a clue where she'd be next year, much less what she wanted to do for the rest of her life. It was enough to get a passing grade in math.

Treena giggled. "You have cheese and sauce all over your face!" She wiped a finger across Amanda's cheek and stuck it into her mouth.

"Eww! That's gross, Treena!"

Treena made a face. "I'll say. It needs more garlic."

She said it so seriously that Amanda started to giggle.

"Principal's coming—run!" a boy yelled from behind them.

Amanda turned around. It was Ravi Sharma—the new kid with the fake hand. Amanda's eyes widened, and her mind buzzed with the recent rumors circulating in the school's hallways. Industrial accident—happened at his father's plastic pail company—chewed off his entire hand—bones crunched, blood spurted everywhere. Now Sharma's artificial hand was covered in tomato sauce, not blood, but Amanda's imagination still ran wild.

"Did you two hear me?" Ravi yelled. "Mrs. Greer's gonna be here any second!"

Amanda shook off her morbid thoughts and looked behind her. The only means of escape was the door leading into the kitchen. Grinning, she glanced back at Treena and Ravi. "Anyone for hide and seek?"

Without waiting for their response, Amanda bolted into the small kitchen the two parent volunteers had deserted. She was immediately followed by the other remaining two food fight fugitives. They yanked open one of the huge cupboard doors, but found it could only fit two.

Amanda flashed Ravi a smile and said, "Ladies first."

"Hey! That's not—" Ravi didn't have time to finish because the kitchen door burst open at the same time as the cupboard door slammed shut.

"Where is she?" Jordan Jensen demanded, still sporting his pizza makeover.

"Where is who?" Ravi asked, whirling around.

"Amanda Sault!"

Through the crack in the cupboard doors, Amanda watched Ravi's lips curl to form a high and mighty smile. She bore down on her teeth and felt them grind.

"What's the matter, Amanda?" Treena whispered. "You look like you've got stage fright."

That was only half the truth. She nudged Treena gently. "Shhhh."

However it was Ravi—the East Indian with an attitude—who was acting up a storm. He inclined his head. "What makes you think she's in here?"

"'Cause I told him I saw you follow her in here," another voice answered from behind Jensen.

Amanda let her view slide from Jordan Jensen wearing clothes that screamed, "I play every sport imaginable"—to the runt lurking behind him. Her face puckered like she had downed a dozen sour candies. It was Drake Bailey, their school's ten-year-old genius. Amanda stared at the two friends, friends who were so different from one another, she couldn't figure out why they were friends in the first place. Jordan loved sports. Drake loved books. Jordan wore anything with a team logo on it. Drake wore oversized clothing plastered with comic book heroes. Jordan was tall, athletic, and blond. Drake was short, smart, and dark. Amanda thumbed her chin. The boys were on opposite ends of the school-cool spectrum, that was for sure.

Everyone in this kitchen was in her grade-eight classroom, where Treena and Jordan sat at the back of the room, while Ravi and Drake sat in the front row. Amanda sat somewhere in the middle—not cool enough for the back, not smart enough for the front. Was this fate or just a bad dream?

Her nose suddenly twitched. Uh oh. Between the general stuffiness of the cupboard and no fresh air getting in, her allergies were begging for release. Amanda covered her nose. *No, no, not now!* Then she jumped, feeling the sting of a sharp pinch. Nope, this wasn't a dream. This was a nightmare.

"Oww! What was that for?" Amanda hissed, rubbing her arm.

"Reality check, girl," Treena whispered. "Your face looks like a zit about to pop."

Amanda's filled her cheeks with air, trying not to laugh.

A high-pitched noise sounding an awful lot like a Taylor Swift song blared from the inside of Treena's purple pants.

Amanda sputtered. "Are you serious?"

Treena grinned, fumbling for her cell phone. "Sure. It could be my agent."

Both cupboard doors were wrenched open. Staring down at them was the orange and scrunched face of Jordan Jensen. With the pizza sauce all over his face, he looked like a deranged cheese doodle. It was too funny. Amanda giggled, and Treena burst into laughter. Jordan's crystal blue eyes zeroed in on Treena.

"What's so funny, Porky Foo Yong?"

Amanda clenched her jaw. Treena being Chinese wasn't the reason Jordan's cruel remark made Amanda's Native American blood boil. He was referring to Treena's body size. Amanda's cheeks burned. It was time to take out the trash.

Jordan Jensen never saw the tackle coming. His head kissed the floor. "Umph! Hey! Get off me, Sault!"

Amanda smirked. "What's the matter, Jensen? Afraid I'll scalp you?"

Drake Bailey jumped her. His short arms wrapped around her neck. Gasping, Amanda reached up, flipped Drake over her head and body slammed him on top of Jordan's chest. Suddenly she felt two pairs of hands haul her away from Drake and Jordan, who still lay flopped over each other. As Treena and Ravi dragged her toward the kitchen door, Amanda got one last kick in.

Jordan and Drake managed to help each other up. Jordan pointed at Amanda, scowling. "If I was you, Sault, I wouldn't leave that trailer park you live in anytime soon!"

"I certainly hope that's not a threat, Mr. Jensen."

Amanda's stomach tightened and her mouth went dry.

In unison, all five heads turned to find Mrs. Greer, White Pines Elementary School's principal, standing in the doorway. With a pinched, militant face, Mrs. Greer pointed toward the double doors.

"The five of you, get in my office! Now!"

2. The Principal's Wrath

*J*ail *would have been better than Grizzly Greer's office,*
Amanda thought as she leaned against the cool blue wall in a
chair in the corner. Her nose flared. The sickly combination of
sweat, sauce, garlic, and cheese almost made her heave. She covered
her nose with her hand and checked the silver clock above Mrs.
Greer's two-toned wooden desk for the third time. The five of them
had been in this hellhole for almost two solid hours. No phone calls.
No lectures. No threats. Just sitting, doing nothing. In a plastic
yellow basket on the far corner of the desk sat four disabled cell
phones of various colors and brands.

Jordan Jensen muttered something incoherent.

"Is there a problem, Jordan?" Mrs. Greer snapped, standing up
behind her desk. She smoothed out her green pantsuit. It was dotted
with pizza sauce.

Jordan licked his bottom lip. "Uh, I was wondering how much
longer we'd be in here? I've got batting practice after school, and
my dad will be ticked if I'm late."

Mrs. Greer smiled that smile at him, the smile a predator flashes
just before consuming its prey. Amanda uncovered her nose, sat up,
and smirked.

"It will take as long as it takes, Jordan," the principal replied curtly.

The phone rang and made them all jump. Mrs. Greer's hand lunged for the receiver with the precision of a striking rattlesnake.

Out of the corner of her eye Amanda saw Drake nudge Jordan. "Do you think we're gonna get suspended for this?" he whispered.

Jordan shrugged, and then glared at Amanda. She averted her eyes to the polished beige floor.

Suspended. Even the sound of that word made her think of the grip Mrs. Greer had on all their throats. Squeezing, squeezing, squeezing, until their eyeballs popped and their heads burst open. *Suspended.* Would she do it? Could she do it? Yes, it was a possibility.

The clicking sound of Mrs. Greer's ruby red nails made Amanda wince. The principal hung up the phone, adjusted her tight bleach-blond hairstyle, and then cleared her throat. "Snack Program is for those of you who don't have a snack in your lunch or didn't have time to eat breakfast. Does everyone understand me so far?"

They all nodded.

"Good. Now that you five understand the concept of the program, I would like you to help me understand something."

"What's that, Mrs. G?" Treena asked with the gusto of a cheerleader. This startled Amanda, who was seated next to her.

Mrs. Greer's mouth curled to the side, revealing her white incisor. "Did you have breakfast this morning, Treena?"

Treena furrowed her brows. She nodded meekly.

"Did you bring a snack?" Mrs. Greer pressed.

Treena shoved her hands in the pouch of her thin pink hoody and nodded again.

Mrs. Greer inclined her head. "It is also my understanding that your parents own the Lucky Goldfish Restaurant. Correct?"

Treena squirmed in her chair and nodded a third time. It was like a snake striking a helpless guinea pig. Amanda could almost hear the squeal, feel the fangs sink in.

"Then—" Mrs. Greer leaned closer to Treena "—do you mind explaining to me why you decided to attend Snack Program?"

Treena suddenly sat up. She removed a hand from her hoody to flick a stray ebony tendril out of her face. "Honestly, Mrs. G, a girl needs a well-balanced diet these days. Do you know what happens when you eat Chinese food for breakfast, Chinese food for lunch, and Chinese food for supper?"

Mrs. Greer's face fell. She stood back and shook her head.

Treena stood and lifted her top to expose her ample belly. "You turn into girly-Buddha."

Laughter flooded the principal's office, with the exception of Mrs. Greer, who remained tight-lipped. She started clicking her nails again. "I don't think you all understand the seriousness of your actions."

The laughter stopped.

"But, Mrs. Greer, it wasn't just us throwing food," Drake explained, his voice cracking.

"Drake's right, Mrs. Greer," Jordan cut in. "We didn't start the food fight. As a matter of fact, if Amanda Sault hadn't hit me with a slice, I wouldn't be sitting here."

Amanda felt her face heat twenty degrees in temperature. She crossed her arms over her chest and dug her nails into her skin so hard that she swore she heard her flesh scream.

"Blaming others, are we, Mr. Jensen?" Mrs. Greer said. "You had a choice to turn the other cheek and simply leave the gym, didn't you?"

"Yeah, but—"

"You're in grade eight, captain of the basketball and baseball teams, and president of the student council," Mrs. Greer cut in. "You above all should know that everyone should be responsible for their own actions."

Responsible. How Amanda hated that word. She bet Jordan did too. It sounded heavy and burdensome—like chains dragging you down. Too bad she couldn't pull out her journal. She had a few choice words to jot down about being responsible. *Try sobering up your mother in time for a job interview, for starters.* Her nails went in deeper, exhuming her thoughts.

Ravi cleared his throat. "Excuse me, Mrs. Greer, but I need to go to the washroom. I'm starting to have phantom pains in my hand."

Startled, Amanda released her grip, sat back and glanced behind Treena. Seated in the middle, Ravi was rubbing his fake right hand like he was in pain. *Real pain.* Navy sleeves covered his arms like they were guarding something secret. Other than its brown skin tone, she had never really gotten a good look at his prosthesis.

Mrs. Greer moved to stand above Ravi. "All right, Ravi, if you insist you need to leave first, then I guess you'll be the one who decides all your fates. What will it be? Detention for the remainder of the school year? Playground clean-up? Or how about suspension?"

"Hey, that bites!" Amanda said. "Ravi shouldn't be made to do that!"

"Excuse me, young lady?" Mrs. Greer whirled around. Her fair brows narrowed, ice blue eyes ready to attack.

Amanda crossed her arms over her orange-splattered overalls, and said, "I agree with Jordan—"

"Oh, that it's your fault?"

Amanda uncrossed her arms. "No. I agree with him that we didn't start it, that's all."

"Well, then, do you mind telling me who *did* start it?" Mrs. Greer asked.

There was a universal code among all students in all schools and White Pines Elementary was no exception. Every student took this oath as if their lives depended on it; never rat on another classmate. It was simple and easy. They all became statues. Amanda just shrugged. She wouldn't tell, none of them would.

"I see. No one seems to know who threw the first slice. Fine," Mrs. Greer said. She turned on her high heels and headed for her desk.

The office went quiet, with the exception of Mrs. Greer rifling through a stack of files.

Amanda cleared her throat. "So...I guess we can go back to class now?"

Mrs. Greer looked up. She had that smile on her face again. Amanda prepared herself to be swallowed whole. "Sorry, Amanda, but you've left me with no other choice but to—"

"I beg your pardon, Mrs. Greer, but may I make a suggestion?"

Amanda blew out some air in relief and turned toward the doorway to face their rescuer. Her face twisted. It was *her*—"the Witch of White Pines."

Mrs. Greer acknowledged her politely. "Of course, Ms. Spencer, what is it?"

The dark-haired woman nodded curtly. "As you know, Mrs. Greer, I volunteer at the Snack Program when time permits. In fact, it was I who made all those fresh pizzas for today. It's really a pity. Nobody had a chance to enjoy my secret homemade tomato sauce."

Amanda puckered her lips. Poison. The sauce was probably pure poison. She was immediately grateful she never ate a piece. Rumors around White Pines whispered that Ms. Spencer practiced witchcraft. She even looked the part with her long black hair and ghoulish green eyes. A thin white streak ran down the left side of her hair, giving her a ghostly appearance. Her flowing floral skirt and white blouse wrapped around her body loosely like an unraveled mummy. She was new to the town—fresh off the boat from England—and moved here because she had inherited the creepy empty house on Center Street. She was way past forty and had never married. Yup, Ms. Spencer was a witch for sure. All that was missing was a black cat and broom.

"So what is your suggestion, Ms. Spencer?" Mrs. Greer asked, fiddling with a pen.

Ms. Spencer smiled. She swept her hand gracefully over Amanda and her four classmates, and said, "I want you to hand them all over to me."

3. *Garden of Evil*

" *A* dults screw up everything," Amanda muttered as she sat on a curb on Center Street, awaiting the four classmates she'd been forced to hang out with for the next two weeks after school. Yard duty. That was their sentence for getting into that stupid food fight. It could have been worse. The Witch of White Pines could have cast a spell and turned them all into toads.

Behind her loomed Ms. Spencer's creepy Victorian house. A sudden chill—the kind you'd get watching a horror movie—made Amanda twist around to see if anyone was lurking there. Beyond a slanted black iron gate, the house glared back at her, threatening. Its various shades of weathered brown and yellow brick resembled a crone's gauzy skin. Her eyes followed the single peak in the middle of the roof and underneath it stood a lone door surrounded by a pointy iron fence. The whole house had that gingerbread look to it, like Hansel and Gretel would emerge screaming, followed closely by the evil, child-eating witch.

Amanda shuddered, and then turned around and continued with her vigilance. She caught movement off to her left by a tall cedar hedge across the street. Its branches quivered like a cornered animal. Then—nothing. She shrugged, dismissing it as a stray cat or the wind.

Amanda sighed. It was now the end of May, and the sun was finally out after a few days of rain. She was thankful for the warmth on her exposed arms. She hugged herself, smelling the fresh scent of cheap detergent clinging to the worn black T-shirt handed down to her by her mother.

"Fortune cookie?"

Amanda practically jumped out of her skin. "Crap, Treena!" she hissed, standing and whirling around. "Are you nuts?"

"No. The last time I checked, I was definitely Chinese," Treena answered with a grin. "Want a fortune cookie or not?"

Amanda stared up at the house of horrors and then glanced at Treena, who was dressed in apple green pants, a Bench brand black hoody, and wedged black sandals. Not your typical work-in-the-garden wear, but Treena was anything but typical. An array of bejeweled barrettes held her shimmering ebony hair in place. Some even matched her earrings. Amanda had opted for a long single braid held in place by a few dollar-store hair bands. It wasn't stylish, but it was practical.

Amanda nodded. "Maybe I should. There's no telling what's gonna happen to us once we pass through that gate."

She grabbed the cookie, cracked it open, and looked at the printed message.

"Well?" Treena asked. "Do we go in or not?"

"It says, *Your future is as boundless as the lofty heavens*," Amanda answered. She crumpled her fortune and stuffed it into her back pocket. "And seeing as it was the choice of suspension or being Ms. Spencer's yard slaves, I'd say our future is bleak if we don't go in."

"Good choice!" Treena cheered.

Together they pushed the rusty gate open. It creaked out a bone-splitting screech.

"Bad choice," Treena groaned.

Amanda patted Treena on the shoulder. "Look, just pretend you're rehearsing for a part in a movie called *Garden of Evil*, and you'll get through this in no time. Okay?"

Treena puckered her lips to one side. "*Garden of Evil?* Hmm…sounds like a juicy part. Okay, sign me up."

Amanda wagged a finger. "You haven't got the part yet. You have to audition."

Treena creased her ebony brows. Amanda watched as she puffed out her cheeks and raised both arms over her head. "Nobody puts Treena Mui in the corner!" she spouted, waving her hands in the air like she was warding off a swarm of wasps. "Not even that witch, Ms. Spencer!"

Amanda clapped. "Congrats. You aced it. You get to go in first."

Treena stopped waving her hands. "Uh, I'd rather be in the supporting role for this movie. You're the star. Ergo—you go in first."

Amanda rolled her eyes. "Fine, I'll lead. Just stop stealing lines from movies."

Treena bowed. "Lead on, Macduff!"

"Huh?"

"It's from *Macbeth*. You know, by Shakespeare—the playwright?"

Amanda rubbed her head. "Great. I'm stuck with MacMui—the dork."

She started to walk past the drooping open gate. Weeds and thistles had sprouted through wide cracks in the cement pathway, and the grass was almost too long to cut with a normal mower. Carcasses of shriveled worms littered the pathway helter-skelter. Considering the ominous setting, Amanda figured that they had been the lucky ones.

"I was just setting the tone for the scene," Treena said. "FYI—*Macbeth* is a tragedy."

"So?" Amanda dodged a huge dandelion.

"So, years ago, something tragic happened at this house."

Amanda sighed. "I'm not playing twenty questions."

"A man got brutally murdered here."

Amanda froze and looked up at the house again. She started to sweat. "Please tell me you're kidding."

"I kid you not. My older brother Tom told me that this place used to be a busy hotel a long time ago. One murder later, it was closed down permanently. And get this, a dismembered hand was found in the yard, but the body was never found. After that, I think two old ladies lived here until they died or disintegrated or something."

Amanda swallowed hard. *This place really is the Garden of Evil.*

"Did you see that?" Treena shrieked, jumping behind her.

Amanda stumbled. "See what?"

"Over there, by those tall bushes with white flowers," Treena said, pointing. "I thought I saw something."

Amanda clenched her teeth and regained her balance. "It was probably a cat."

"No, no. It was definitely bigger than a housecat. More like a mountain lion."

"Stop being such a drama queen!" Amanda grabbed Treena by the arm and hauled her toward the house. Arriving on the sagging white porch, she gathered her courage, rapped on the front door, and waited. No answer.

"Darn, no one's home, let's go." Treena turned on her sandals.

"Hold it. We should check the backyard just in case. You don't want Mrs. Greer hearing we were a no-show, do you?"

Treena shook her head. "Hey, speaking of no-shows, where are the guys?"

Amanda shrugged. "Dunno. I thought they'd be here by now. Maybe they're still waiting for Drake at the cemetery."

Treena's almond-shaped eyes bugged. "Cemetery? Why?"

Amanda looked at her strangely. "You do know his mom died, right?"

"Yeah, but that was over a year ago."

"He's only ten, Treena. Remember, he skipped three grades? Plus his dad's been posted to the Middle East again, so he's probably missing her even more. I heard his grandma is staying with him until his dad gets home—whenever that is."

Treena went quiet, digesting this. A sudden gust of wind delivered a strong fragrance to Amanda. It wasn't floral or the scent of grass. It was a more earthy odor—like something had just been dug up. Then, Amanda remembered the missing body Treena had mentioned. Her nose flared, itched, and then let loose. She sneezed all over Treena.

"Eww! Really?" Treena's face twisted. "Next time, use your sleeve!"

Amanda sniffed. "Sorry. Allergies."

"There are pills for that," Treena replied haughtily, shaking her hoody as if she had received a bad case of the cooties.

Amanda rolled her eyes. She gripped Treena's shoulder. "Come on. There's probably a hose you can wash up with in the back."

It took five minutes to hop the porch, weave through the jungle of bushes and shrubs, and detach themselves from some sharp rose

24

thorns. Squatting behind what Amanda thought was a lilac bush, the two classmates peered out into the backyard. It was massive. Massive and overgrown—like another world existed inside it. They heard something crack behind them. The girls turned around. A disfigured ape-like creature with stringy black hair and enormous fangs teetered over them like it was deciding who to eat first. A bloodied eye—complete with bulbous veins—was perched precariously on its mashed-in nose. Hairy hands sprouted from a long sleeved black shirt.

"Baahaahaahaa!" it shrieked.

The girls screamed. Treena grabbed Amanda and pulled her into the closest bush with the thickest foliage. They both squirmed, their feet digging into the ground in a desperate attempt to escape, while branches and leaves snagged their hair and scraped their faces. Amanda flinched as she felt the sticky threads of a spider's web float across her cheek.

Through the leaves and gnarled branches, she could see the shaggy beast. It suddenly stopped swaying and slowly shucked off its hairy hands. Then, it reached up to pull off its deformed head. Amanda's eyes widened. It was Ravi Sharma. He grinned, then winked at them. Amanda clenched her fists. It was time to add a ripe black eye to his real face.

Jordan and Drake stood behind Ravi, resembling campy *Children of the Corn* knock-offs in old plaid shirts and jeans, laughing like a couple of crazy coyotes. Then, Amanda caught a dark, shimmering movement behind the boys. She frowned. Whatever it was had no definite shape, as if it were a demented amoeba. It broke through a clump of waist-high shrubs and landed behind Jordan, Drake, and Ravi. Treena squealed, hugged Amanda tighter, and pulled them both deeper into the bushes. Amanda puffed her cheeks, her arms flailing like branches fighting off the wind. The blackish-green creature thrashed back and forth. Its thin leathery tail whipped about wildly. Two metal claws protruding from its belly lashed out.

"Eeeyah! Eeeyah! Eeeyah!" it wailed.

It was the boys' turn to scream. They were trapped with nowhere to go.

From deep inside the bushes, Amanda watched Ravi drop his monster mask and bolt through a patch of rose bushes, heading toward a cluster of thick shrubbery covered with twisted vines. It would have been a perfect hiding place if the branches bent like they did for the breeze, but they didn't. Instead, he tripped over a root and slammed head-first into the ground. Amanda winced, feeling the *whump* of Ravi's landing vibrate through her.

"Ravi! Are you okay?" Jordan asked, running toward him.

Amanda pushed her way out of the bushes. She sprinted over to join Jordan. Ravi groaned and rolled himself on to his back, looking like a body in a coffin. A lump the size of an eagle's egg protruded from his forehead. Amanda grimaced. *Maybe Ravi should put his mask back on.*

He licked his lips and moaned. "S-S-Sorry, Dad. I-I shouldn't have put my hand in the machine."

"Dad? Ravi, it's me, Jordan. What are you talking about?"

Ravi's eyes flew open. He sat up and pushed Jordan away. "Nothing! I'm good! Leave me alone!"

Jordan stumbled and backed off. "Hey, I was just making sure you didn't get a concussion, dude!"

"Is he okay?"

Amanda turned to her right. It was Treena, fresh out of the forest with enough leaves and twigs stuck in her hair to start a campfire. Most of her barrettes were missing. Dirt was smeared across her cheeks, and her expensive hoody looked as if she'd found it in a dumpster instead of a high-end clothing store.

"He'll survive," Jordan replied. "Not so sure about his mental state."

Treena nodded, then snatched up a pail of water sitting next to a budding shrub. She looked down at Ravi and grinned. "My, you look a little fried after your jog through the jungle, Ravi. How about something to cool you down?"

Before Ravi could answer, Treena doused him with the water.

"A-A-Are you crazy? Do you know how much this hand costs?" Ravi sputtered, covering up his prosthesis. Then he glared at Treena. "You're gonna pay for that, Buddha-butt!"

"That's quite enough!" It was the shiny green creature. And it was standing behind them. There was no escaping now.

Suddenly, its belly shook, as if getting ready to spill its guts all over them. Amanda prepared to be splattered by green entrails any second. The metal claws savagely tore through the thin tissue, as a human hand appeared to rip away the rest of its skin. To Amanda's surprise, Ms. Spencer emerged from her ghoulish cocoon, looking very much like the Bride of Frankenstein.

Ms. Spencer smoothed her witchy dark hair back in place, and then stepped out of her green costume. It had only been a huge, plastic garbage bag along with a couple of three-pronged garden tools for hands and a garden hose for the tail. She wagged her finger at the lot of them, and said, "If you children continue to act no better than wild apes, then I'll be forced to have a talk with your principal. Do you really want that?"

Everyone shook their heads. Nobody wanted to deal with Grizzly Greer.

"Good," Ms. Spencer said approvingly. Then she looked down and her face turned ashen.

"Oh…my…goodness!" She swooped down on Ravi. Her long fingers pushed down on his forehead. He winced.

"Does that hurt?" she asked.

Ravi scowled and tried to shrug her off, but Ms. Spencer held him like a python. "It does when you poke at it!"

"Awesome!" Drake blurted. "That's one sick bump on your head, Ravi!"

Amanda nodded. "Betcha that'll leave a mark."

"Now you don't need to wear any of your monster masks," Treena said with a smirk. "I'd say you've found the perfect look."

They all laughed, with the exception of Ms. Spencer. She was still attacking Ravi's forehead with her sharp fingernails. Amanda noticed Ravi's face getting redder and redder, as if he were a volcano about to explode. He finally broke free of Ms. Spencer's grip.

"Leave me alone!" he screamed. "I'm a man!"

"Can we take a vote on that?" Treena asked, putting up her hand.

Ravi glared at her, rolled away from Ms. Spencer, and made an awkward attempt to stand. Wobbly on his feet, he turned to jump over the shrubs he'd tried to hurdle earlier, but his foot got snagged in the gnarled vines surrounding the shrubs, and ripped off his shoe. He fell again. This time, he managed to tear away a clump of branches from the shrubs. Amanda shook her head. It was like watching Wile E. Coyote trying to escape his own traps. She could almost hear the Road Runner go "beep beep" in victory.

"Oh! Ravi, are you all right?" Ms. Spencer shrieked, dropping to her knees by his side. She propped him up on her lap. His damp head came to rest upon her long, tan skirt, and this time, he surrendered.

Trying not to laugh at Sharma's karma, Amanda walked over to retrieve his shoe for him, and caught a glimpse of something partially revealed under the mass of greenery. She squinted. "What's that?" Amanda asked, pointing. "There...under those vines and branches that Ravi tripped over."

Ms. Spencer looked where Amanda was pointing, and gasped. She stretched to pull away some plant debris. Whatever it was, it was made of stone and it looked as though it had been there a long time.

"It...it can't possibly be, can it?" Ms. Spencer whispered, as her brow furrowed and the corners of her eyes crinkled.

Amanda smelled a sharp humus odor. Her nose wrinkled, but didn't itch. It was that earthy smell again. She closed her eyes and took deeper whiff. There was decaying freshness to it, as if something was alive underneath the layers of soil. The sound of grunting and huffing brought Amanda out of her sensory stupor. She opened her eyes. Drake and Jordan were both at work, tearing away the shrubs, branches, and vines.

"Can't be what?" Ravi asked weakly.

Ms. Spencer didn't answer. Whatever *it* was seemed to have a grip on her throat.

Treena nudged Amanda and passed her one of the three-pronged garden tools Ms. Spencer used for claws. "Let's make like Indiana Jones and dig this puppy out!"

Following Treena's lead, Amanda knelt on the thick carpet of grass and weeds and struck the earth, again and again, digging as if there was a vein of gold underneath them. As more of the stone object was revealed, she noted that strange, ancient-looking symbols were carved all over it. Most of the designs were foreign to her, with the exception of some engraved spirals. Wiping sweat from her brow, Amanda wondered how tall it was. Her height? Twice her height? It was hard to tell. Moss had acted like layers of chewing gum, invading crevices within the stone, while the color, the dirtiest of gray, had a definite dullness to it. It resembled a forgotten tombstone, left to disintegrate with time.

"Awesome!" Drake yelled. "This thing must be thousands of years old!"

"Get a grip, Drake," Jordan said. "It's probably an old lawn ornament."

Drake snorted. He scraped some moss away from the stone. "Look, this is an Egyptian hieroglyphic. You know, like the writing you'd see on the walls of the pyramids."

"I'd say too many of your genius brain cells are colliding with all those comic books you read," Jordan replied. He hunkered down and pointed to another engraving. "Some history freak must have carved these symbols, either for a joke or to make it look authentic for some reason. It's the only explanation."

"You've been hit in the head one too many times with a football," Drake spat, balling his fists. "I'm smart enough to know what's fake and what's real, and these symbols happen to be the real deal, brain-drain!"

Jordan stood up. "Listen, my Uncle John is into all this historical junk, and he's taught me about the ancient Egyptians. If this was real, why would symbols like this pitchfork—" he pointed to the middle part of the exposed stone "—be carved on it? It's not something you'd see in a pyramid. Answer that one, boy-genius!"

Amanda stood, backed away, and waited for Drake to go for Jordan's belly button. However, it was Ms. Spencer, still kneeling and coddling Ravi, who would slay Drake's dragon.

"Drake is correct, Jordan. It is thousands of years old," she answered while wiping dirt from Ravi's brow with the tip of her skirt. "At least twelve thousand years, by my calculation."

4. *Ancient Secrets*

*A*manda's jaw dropped. *Twelve thousand years old?* She shook her head. *Impossible.* The lady must have added something other than milk and sugar to her afternoon tea. Amanda arched a brow and glanced down at the strange stone whatever-it-was. It did look ancient. Especially with all those Egyptian symbols etched into it. So what was it doing buried in Ms. Spencer's backyard, underneath an overgrown mound of cedars, shrubs, and vines? Her inquiring mind needed to know.

"So...are you gonna keep us in suspense, Ms. Spencer?" Amanda asked, tossing the garden tool aside. She walked over to the exposed stone and began digging out a chunk of soft moss from an engraved spiral with her finger.

"I-I beg your pardon?" Ms. Spencer replied, as if she'd been beamed back to earth.

"You seem to know what this is. Care to share?" Amanda flicked the moss in the shrubs and went for seconds.

Treena joined Amanda in her quest to eradicate the vegetation, only she used the three-pronged garden tool. Scraping and digging, Treena suddenly stopped and looked at Amanda the way a hungry archeologist would.

"Wow, I bet this thing is worth a lot of money."

"Actually…it's priceless," Ms. Spencer said. Then she took a deep breath. "And please, since we'll be seeing a lot of each other during the next two weeks, I want you all to call me Melody."

Amanda was fine with that. She just wanted answers. "So, Ms. Spenc—uh, Melody, if this thing is worth a lot, why has it been buried and left to disintegrate in your backyard?"

Before Melody Spencer could answer Amanda, Drake rushed over and grabbed the garden tool out of Treena's hand. "Careful, Treena, don't scrape away any of the glyphs! This could be some kind of ancient stele."

"Glyphs? Stele?" Treena replied indignantly. "Talk in a language we can all understand, Bailey."

Drake rolled his eyes. "Glyphs are all those carvings in the stone, and each one means something. A stele is a kind of marker that tells us things. You know, like a gravestone or—"

"Eww! You mean somebody could be buried under this thing?" Treena squealed. She scrunched her face and ran behind Melody and Ravi.

"Hey, maybe it's the person who was murdered here when this place used to be a hotel," Jordan said. Then he looked down at it and started to slowly back away.

"No, no, no!" Drake shook his head wildly. "This isn't a gravestone. The hieroglyphics don't mention death anywhere."

"Don't tell me you know how to read ancient Egyptian writing," Amanda said haughtily. "I'll puke if you do."

Drake grinned. "Treena, toss Amanda that bucket you doused Ravi with. I think she's gonna need it."

Amanda's face twitched. Great. The little toady loser could read ancient scribbling. She puckered her lips to one side and said, "So what's it say then, brainiac?"

"Just one moment," Melody said.

She checked the goose egg on Ravi's forehead once more and then lifted him up off the long grass. He stumbled, but she held him firmly, and then started to pick garden debris out of his ebony hair.

"How are you feeling now, Ravi?" Melody asked softly.

"Better. Thanks, Ms.—I mean, Melody," Ravi replied, checking his bump.

Amanda could see he was still a little shaky.

Melody nodded. "Good. I'll get you some ice to put on that bump in a few minutes. In the meantime, Treena, will you please make sure he doesn't fall again?"

Treena pursed her lips as if mulling it over, then winked at Melody. "Sure, Melody. If Ravi has one more fall, he'll be a shoo-in for a job as a crash-test dummy."

Melody stifled a giggle under her breath while brushing dead leaves from her skirt. She walked toward Amanda and Drake, then bent down to inspect one of the engravings.

"It's not a stele, Drake. It's something much more," She said, her slender fingers tracing the chosen glyph over and over again.

"Much more? What do you mean, Ms.—um, Melody?" Drake asked.

Melody stopped tracing and looked up at Drake. "If my great aunt's journals prove to be correct, this could very well be the top portion of an ancient stone arch. In one of her journals she wrote that for a period of time, this arch was a gateway to unlimited riches."

Amanda smiled. She liked the sound of that. Riches. Unlimited riches. "What kind of riches?Gold? Jewels? Money? A lifetime membership to Chuck E. Cheese?"

Melody pursed her lips. "No, no, not *those* kind of riches, Amanda. Apparently, this arch contains ancient secrets that humankind has yet to understand, let alone acknowledge. At least that's what I've read so far in her journals. There must be dozens of them in the library."

"Ancient secrets?" Treena scratched her chin, then smiled. "Tell us more!"

"There's really not much to tell, Treena. I've been too busy sorting out everything in the house that I haven't had the time to read through the journals I've found so far, much less venture into the garden. That's why the yard is such a mess. My great aunt—her name was Florence Whitney—died last winter, and as I was her only living relative, I inherited the lot, as well as the debt and needed repairs that went with it." Melody looked up into the sky. "Thanks a bunch, Aunt Flo."

Jordan laughed. "I bet whoever sold that arch to dear old Aunt Flo saw her coming. She got conned big time!"

Melody frowned. "She didn't buy it, Jordan. The house's previous owners, Max and Frances Tarbush did. In Aunt Florence's oldest journal she wrote that the Tarbushes had purchased the stone arch sometime in nineteen hundred from an Egyptian antiquity dealer who bragged it was eight thousand years older than the pyramids. He sweetened the deal by sharing that there were ancient secrets scrawled all over it. The Tarbushes saw the potential for the stone arch to become a tourist attraction for their flourishing hotel, so they bought it. Apparently it took over ten men to put it in place."

"Wait, there's no logic here, Melody," Drake blurted. "If this arch is eight thousand years older than the pyramids, then what was it doing in the possession of that antiquity dealer? Either the dude was sleazy and pulling a fast one on the Tarbushes or—"

"Or it's all true," Melody cut in. "The dealer may have known what he had all along and wanted to profit from it in any way he could."

"Yeah, that makes sense," Treena said. "He wouldn't have gotten a penny or a drachma or whatever they used for money back then if the arch went to a museum."

Ravi whistled. "Yeah, and maybe he was selling it for some slimy tomb robbers who scored it from looting a pyramid." Then he stared at the arch for a second and took a few steps back. Amanda watched Ravi's face tic. "Maybe it's cursed. Maybe that's why it's buried. So no one will find it. But we found it. Oh, no. Guys, I think we're in big trouble."

"Cut the crap, Sharma," Jordan said. "Why would the arch get buried and forgotten if it's full of ancient secrets and unlimited riches? That's the part I don't get."

"I can't believe I'm agreeing with Jordan, but he's right, Ravi," Amanda said, as she pushed her long, single braid off her shoulder. "There's a reason someone wanted the arch hidden. We just have to figure out what it is."

"What else did you find out from Aunt Flo's journals, Melody?" Drake asked.

She brushed her hands against her tan skirt, and then stood up. She sighed. "Well, I hadn't realized my great aunt came over here as a home child from England when she was quite young, and was eventually adopted by Francis Tarbush."

"What's a home child?" Treena asked.

Drake snorted. "It's another form of child slavery."

"Pretty much, Drake," Melody said. "Shipping poor or orphaned children to foreign countries to forcibly work in homes or on farms is nothing short of barbaric. Although I do believe that my great aunt was one of the lucky ones. While growing up here she had managed to decipher some of the arch's hieroglyphics, most of which were simple recipes to cure certain sicknesses. But some cures—" she paused to lick her bottom lip "—used different healing remedies like colored crystals and sound. Aunt Florence wrote that she experimented with this crystal treatment and became quite adept at it. It's possible she was ahead of her time."

"Or maybe she was a witch," Amanda blurted. "It seems to run in the family."

Amanda's classmates stared at her. All mouths but Ravi's fell open. His face started to tic again. Okay, maybe she had been to-the-point and blunt. But talk around town insinuated that Melody Spencer was a bona fide, true-blue hex-machine from England. Amanda suddenly felt the need to take a step back but couldn't because the unearthed portion of the twelve-thousand-year-old arch was blocking her path. She gulped, tasting bile. Maybe it was time to vomit after all.

However, Melody seemed unfazed, like she couldn't care less what Amanda had suggested. Without taking her fierce green eyes off Amanda, Melody slowly crossed her arms over her cotton blouse and said, "So you think I'm a witch, do you, Amanda?"

Amanda nodded. It was all she could do because her teeth were frozen shut. At least she had been the brave one. Everybody else remained tight-lipped.

Melody's face turned serious. "Listening to rumors not only poisons the soul, but also seeps into the garden of the mind. Just because I do things differently from others doesn't mean I should be stigmatized. I'm an herbalist. I practice healing by using herbs, as I'm sure your ancestors did years ago, and may still do."

Amanda's chin dropped to her chest. Melody was right. Even her grandmother, a full-blooded Ojibwa, preferred to use certain plants to heal cuts and take pain away. Okay, maybe she had jumped the canoe on this one. But what about those weird night rituals Amanda had heard that Melody Spencer performed? Herbs just didn't cut it.

Amanda lifted her chin. "Then explain why I heard you've been seen reciting weird poetry and lighting candles outside whenever there's a full moon?"

Melody laughed. It was actually a musical laugh, like a wind chime coming alive in the breeze. "I celebrate every full moon, as well as every new season. It's just my way of embracing change and welcoming new things to come, Amanda. It's no different than saying a prayer or mantra, and there's nothing wrong with how I choose to live my life as long as I'm not hurting myself or anyone. I've learned that people fear what they don't understand. Maybe that's the reason why this stone arch was buried and hidden away in Aunt Florence's garden. Maybe, deep down, she knew people weren't ready for the kind of knowledge and secrets it held."

Amanda's balloon burst. "I...I guess I owe you an apology. Sorry, Melody."

Melody smiled and walked over to Amanda. Amanda felt the wall disappear between them the moment Melody hugged her. "On the contrary, Amanda, if you don't ask questions, you'll never know the truth. Do you see?"

Amanda nodded. There was something soothing about being in Melody's embrace. Witch or no witch, the woman cast a spell over Amanda in that moment.

Melody briskly patted Amanda on the back and stepped away. "Good. Now, Drake, did you say that you could interpret these hieroglyphics?"

Drake cracked his knuckles and nodded. "I'll give it my best shot, Melody."

Melody raised a dark brow. She tapped Drake under the chin, and pointed down to the exposed portion of the arch. "What does it say under the carved-out trident?" she asked.

Amanda followed Melody's finger. She squinted. Melody was talking about the pitchfork that Jordan had spoken of earlier. It was etched in the top middle section they had uncovered, and was about the size of a bookmark. It looked like a three-pronged spear a fisherman would use. Underneath this trident were four small, slightly slanted Egyptian symbols flecked with moss. Boy-genius was silent for the moment. His brain must have gone into overdrive because he was usually quick with answers. Using the air as if it were a piece of paper, Drake started drawing out shapes and symbols. He scrunched his face, muttered something to himself, shook his head, and then pulled out his cell phone.

Tapping it a few times, Drake's fingers flew across the screen. Mumbling, he nodded once, twice, three times before shoving his phone back in the side pocket of his baggy pants.

Amanda rolled her eyes. "Well? Do I puke or not?"

Drake smirked. He kicked the bucket toward Amanda. "I'm positive it says, *Time flows through us.*"

5. *Professor Lucas*

*T*he annoying ringtone of the National Hockey League's anthem sounded again, making a total of six times. Amanda checked Jordan Jensen's shiny red cell phone again. She frowned. It was Ashley Prigham sending another text. This would be the fourth since Amanda had found the phone by the bike stand at school, twenty minutes ago. She looked at Jordan's cell. *What u doing?* Amanda rolled her eyes. She wanted to respond, *get a life, douche,* but didn't. Instead, she turned it off.

Normally Amanda would have waited until she met up with Jordan at Melody 's place, but two urgent messages from his mom made her decide to take a detour toward his house on Oak Street to give Jordan his phone back and tell him to call his mom. She stuffed the cell down the pocket of her worn jean overalls, now speckled with light orange blotches from the infamous food fight. She sighed. Their two-week yard detention was almost up, and then life as she knew it would go back to being the same. Boring. Uneventful. Fighting with Mom.

Thankfully, her mother had managed to keep a job waitressing for the restaurant near the car plant for the last three months. Good. At least the tips paid the utilities, and there was food in the fridge. As Amanda rounded the corner, she could see Jordan's picture-perfect house nestled among a couple of oak trees. The two-story red brick home hosted a manicured lawn and several perennial gardens with an occasional ceramic gnome peering out from under a bush. A silver mountain bike was propped up against the white garage door, one pedal still spinning.

As Amanda walked up to Jordan's driveway, she gripped the straps on her blue nylon backpack until her fingers ached. Her white T-shirt started to cling to her skin, so she pulled at the neckline with one hand. The closer she got to the house, the stronger the smell of fresh driveway sealer got. Deciding to detour, she leaped onto the grass, fresh shavings catching between her sandals and feet, and headed toward the front door. Taking out Jordan's phone, Amanda knocked on the door. A full minute went by before she rapped on the door again. No answer. She repeated, only with more force. The door suddenly flew open, and Amanda's fist connected with Jordan's chin.

Startled, Amanda dropped the cell phone.

"Oww!" Jordan flinched. He cupped his chin.

"S-Sorry, Jordan!" Amanda stammered. "It was an accident!"

"Save it!" he snapped. Then Jordan looked down. His eyes widened. "Hey, my cell phone! I've been looking for it everywhere! Where'd you find it?"

"You dropped it by the bike stand. It slipped out of your pocket as you left. Thought you might want it, seeing you're as attached to that as you are to a limb. Call your mom. It's important. Something about working late and your uncle."

There. Message delivered. Her appearance explained.

"My uncle?" Jordan bent down to retrieve his phone. He turned it on and started to check his messages.

She waved. "See you at Melody's."

"Wait, Amanda," Jordan blurted. "Um, come in, we…we might as well walk over together."

Amanda furrowed her brows. She eyed Jordan carefully. His tawny hair was more tousled than usual, his blue eyes sincere. He was still wearing the clothes he'd worn at school—a purple T-shirt, black track pants, and the latest sport shoe on the market. The smell of homemade apple pie lured her in, until she noticed it was only a decorative candle on the hall table.

"I don't bite."

Amanda jumped. Then she smirked. "Yeah, but you do bark."

Jordan laughed. "Gimme a minute to see what my mom wanted and we'll go."

Amanda nodded as he ran down the hall. Then she noticed the contents of Jordan's black backpack strewn across the floor. *Nice,* she thought. *He's as messy as Mom.* She looked around. Honey-colored hardwood floors, light bronze walls—close to the color of her skin—and an assortment of needlepoint pictures made her feel welcome. But it was the finely-crafted carpet woven in colors of chocolate brown, pumpkin orange, and whipped-cream white that nourished her insides thoroughly.

Sighing, Amanda kicked off her sandals, dropped her bag to the floor, and padded over to Jordan's backpack. She tipped it upright, its open mouth resembling a hungry baby bird's, and started to fill it with the stuff scattered on the floor. A couple of text books, a large purple hooded sweatshirt, a mini pair of binoculars, pens, a binder, and—she made a face—his jockstrap. Grabbing for a pen, she gingerly lifted it up off the floor and flicked it into the bag.

"Eww, eww, eww," Amanda muttered, throwing the pen aside. Then she spied a photo under the table and reached for it.

It was a digital print Treena had taken this week of Melody's twelve-thousand-year-old stone arch. Amanda smiled. Her thumb grazed the glossy photo, remembering how it had only taken them a few days to unearth it. Melody had even rented a small bulldozer to pull the seven foot tall arch back into its original standing position. Once that milestone was completed, they all put in a lot of elbow grease to clean it up. Drake had done some research to find out what kind of chemicals were needed to buff up the stone and get rid of all the brown and green stains it had accumulated throughout the years of neglect.

The stone arch now shone like dappled marble, flecked with tones of brown, white, and gray. Most of the hieroglyphics had been preserved and were now legible. Besides the trident in the keystone Jordan had recognized earlier, a group of seven spirals had been carved into the arch. To Amanda, both the trident and spirals looked out of place, like they didn't belong with the rest of the ancient scribbling. Drake had been puzzled by a line of glyphs that mentioned the "old red land" and could offer no explanation. Imagine that, the boy-genius was stumped!

Melody, on the other hand, had become certain that the stone arch was some type of library that held precious secrets and knowledge to the past. Every night, she hungrily read her great aunt's journals to look for any clues. But so far she had come up empty-handed.

"Hello?"

Amanda jumped. She clutched the photo to her chest and turned around slowly. A man stood in the doorway. Wearing jeans and a rumpled beige button-down shirt, he looked as if he could have passed for the winning contestant on *Survivor*, except that his face was clean shaven. His age was a mystery, but Amanda put him in his forties. Without making a move, she watched as he raked a large tanned hand through his thick, shoulder-length sandy hair. Suddenly, the strong fumes of his spicy cologne ambushed Amanda in the hallway. She sneezed, and sneezed again.

"*Gesundheit,*" the man said, as he sauntered in, carrying an over-stuffed duffle bag.

Amanda rubbed her nose. "Huh?"

"*Gesundheit* means to wish you good health. Probably stems from the Middle Ages during the bubonic plague." He stopped and eyed her. "Unless, by chance, you sneezed because you're vulnerable to evil spirits?"

"No. Just allergies," Amanda replied, looking at him strangely.

The man laughed. He tossed his duffle bag aside, almost knocking over the hall table. "I'm John Lucas, Leslie's brother." He held out his hand, callused and pitted with scars.

"Who's Leslie?" she asked suspiciously, still clutching the photo.

The man withdrew his hand. "Leslie Jensen. Jordan's mother. You must be a friend of his, since you're about his age. Unless—"

"Unless what?" Amanda asked.

"Unless, you're his new girlfriend," he said with a wink.

Like an oven set to broil, Amanda's entire insides heated up. Her cheeks gushed white hot. Her armpits felt soaked, and her throat closed up. Without realizing it, Amanda crumpled the photo into a ball.

"Uncle John!" Jordan shouted from down the hall.

"Hey, Tiger!"

Jordan sprinted down the hallway as if he were entering a cheering stadium. Then, he skidded to a stop. His mouth fell open as soon as he saw his uncle.

"Is there a problem, Jordan?"

Jordan continued to stare at his uncle as if he were under a spell.

"Is my fly low or something?" He checked his zipper.

Jordan blinked. "Wow! Did you get a cool-dude make-over or something? You're not wearing your usual geeky polyester professor gear."

His uncle shot him a lopsided smile. "Cute. I guess you could say my lifestyle has changed somewhat."

"Did you finally meet a woman? Is she hot?"

Amanda stifled a giggle.

"No, I did not meet a woman! Honestly, Jordan. That sounds like something your mother would say, with the exception of that 'hot' crack."

"Er, sorry, my bad," Jordan replied.

He smiled. "So, are you going to introduce me to your girlfr—"

"I'm Amanda Sault," Amanda blurted, cutting him off. "Um, I'm in Jordan's class."

"Study buddies?" he pressed.

"Ahh, no, more like—" Amanda paused, unsure how to define their relationship.

"Wait a sec, aren't you supposed to be teaching at Notre Dame?" Jordan asked, breaking Amanda's awkward stall tactic.

He nodded. Amanda noticed that his sky blue eyes suddenly glazed over.

Jordan must have noticed it too. "What's wrong?"

He shrugged. "Nothing you can fix, Tiger. Unless, by chance, you can pull a once-in-a-lifetime ancient discovery out of a magician's black hat for me."

Jordan leaned against the wall. "You've lost me."

"That's okay, Jordan. I'm a little lost myself these days. To make a long story short, I've been disgraced, discredited, and suspended from my teaching responsibilities at Norte Dame for an indefinite period of time, thanks to Marcus Crowley."

Jordan frowned. "Who?"

"Professor Marcus Crowley—my star protégé in the study of ancient cultures. He was thirsty to learn, so I took him under my wing and taught him everything I knew. It ended up he was smarter, and sneakier, than I thought. And it was a bone-head move on my part."

"What exactly did he do to you?" Jordan asked as he checked his wrist-watch. Amanda glanced over his shoulder. It was just after four. They had to be at Melody's house by four-thirty.

"Am I keeping you and Amanda from something important, Jordan?"

Jordan looked up. "Sort of. A bunch of us got in trouble at school, and for punishment were given yard duty. No biggie. So...are you gonna tell me what this Crowley jerk did?"

Jordan's uncle sighed, wiped his mouth with the back of his hand, and said, "That back-stabber stole most of my research as well as a rare Mayan artifact we found during an archeological dig in Central America early this spring. For the life of me, I still don't know how he moved the thing. It must weigh close to five tons or better. When all the dust settled, I was the one held responsible. At first, I was thrown in jail. But, because of my position at Notre Dame, I was bailed out and sent home, where I was asked by the University Board to take an extended leave while things were cleared up with the authorities in Guatemala. Apparently, they don't take too kindly to looters."

Jordan shrugged. "Can you still teach?"

He nodded. "Eventually. I'm still a professor, if that counts for anything."

"I guess you've been given a detention too," Jordan said. Then he grinned. "We must be related!"

He rumpled Jordan's tawny hair. "I'll tell you what, when you and Amanda are finished with your yard obligations, the three of us will go out for some burgers and fries."

Stunned at the invitation, Amanda released the crinkled photo. It bounced off her foot and rolled toward Jordan's uncle.

"I'll get it,," he said, bending.

He picked the photo up, began smoothing it out, and then stopped. His jaw dropped. "What...the...hell?"

Jordan frowned. "Is something wrong?"

"It's...it's impossible," Jordan's uncle muttered.

"Huh? What's impossible?"

He continued to stare at the photo, his face void of expression.

Jordan poked his uncle. "Earth to Uncle. Come in, Uncle."

Suddenly, his breathing became raspy, almost asthmatic.

Amanda's stomach knotted. Something about the way the professor stared at the picture unnerved her, spooked her. She took a step back.

"Do you want me to call Mom?" Jordan asked in a worried tone.

Jordan's uncle didn't answer. Instead, he straightened up, clamped the photo between his teeth, then reached for his duffle bag on the floor and ripped it open. He started pulling out articles of clothing and books, throwing them all over the floor until he came across a blue twill bucket hat decorated with an assortment of fishing lures. He plopped it on his head, then turned toward Jordan and roughly grabbed his shoulder. Jordan winced as his uncle removed the photo of the stone arch from his teeth, and shoved it under Jordan's nose.

"Show me where this is, Jordan! Now!" he demanded.

Amanda's whole body tightened, and her mouth went soupy. An invisible wall went up between the nutty professor and herself. He had transformed into someone obsessive, demanding, controlling, right before her eyes—all because of that photo. Amanda's survival instinct kicked in. She needed to warn the others. *Run. Get out. Go.*

6. The Crystal Key

manda was lucky to get out of Jordan's house alive. She snatched up her sandals and backpack, and flew out the front door before Jordan's crazy-eyed uncle could nab her. She tried to shake off her fear. Professor Lucas had freaked her out. His actions, his voice, his manner reminded her of a psychotic man her mom had once dated. Amanda shuddered just thinking about him. She licked her lips and swallowed a sour ball of guilt. Poor Jordan was still in there, cornered like a cat against a coyote.

Desperate times called for desperate measures, so Amanda stole Jordan's bike. She'd gotten three streets over before she realized that she'd mistakenly also taken his backpack. Breathing hard, Amanda continued on, rounding another road, until she spotted Melody 's house. *Go, go, go, almost there.* Pumping, pumping, pumping the pedals, her legs ached while her lungs gave silent thanks, as she skidded to a stop, jumped off the bike, and let it fall into a patch of crabgrass past the gate.

She headed for the backyard. *I've got to get to the others before he does.*

As Amanda rounded the corner of the house, she tripped over a rake and landed in a garden bed of freshly turned soil. *Whump!* With a nostril full of dirt, Amanda wiped her nose and shook her head.

Disoriented, she looked around. Melody, Drake, and Treena were standing on the sagging back porch. It creaked, its tired foundation protesting under their weight.

"Look what I found last night, kids," Melody announced in a whimsical voice.

Drake whistled. "That's wicked-awesome, Melody!"

"OMG! Let me see it, let me touch it!" Treena squealed.

The sun caught what Melody handed to Treena and Amanda winced at its brightness. She hooded her eyes with a hand to get a better look and saw that it was a crystal trident, about the size of a pen.

"Where'd you find it?" Drake asked, sliding his knapsack off his shoulder and dumping it on the porch. The porch creaked again.

"Believe it or not, Drake, I discovered it inserted inside the front cover of an antiquated-looking book. The book had been concealed within a secret compartment behind one of the bookshelves in the library. It must be important, or Aunt Florence wouldn't have gone to all that trouble to hide it."

Treena traced a finger up and down the clear prongs of the trident. "Does the book tell you what this crystal trident is used for?"

"I'm not sure yet. It seems the book was written in sets of abstruse riddles, as if it's only intended for someone specific, someone who would understand what all the gibberish means."

"A book of riddles?" Drake said. "Sounds like something Nostradamus would pull."

Melody sighed. "I'm sure it would take a prophet like him to reveal the mysteries hidden in the book."

Treena continued to run her finger up and down the prongs, faster and faster, until it started making a high-pitched ringing sound. She stopped. "Whoa, do you hear that?"

"Sounds like an angel singing," Melody replied.

Drake covered his ears. "More like a couple of hummingbirds fighting."

Before Amanda could interrupt, her heart started to race.

"Hmm, I wonder what would happen if you did—" Treena tapped the wooden railing with the crystal trident "—this?"

Amanda's ears rang with an intensity she had never known before. A queasy, sick feeling ambushed her entire body. Her mouth went dry. She wanted to throw up, but couldn't, needed to sweat,

48

but didn't. It felt like her body was awakening, connecting to her in a language she didn't understand. Something deep inside her echoed, calling to her in a strange yet familiar way. She forced herself to look at the crystal trident in Treena's hand, and then, as if it spoke to her, to look at the recently resurrected stone arch in the middle of the yard. She turned her head, and like the sparkling trident, it too, glistened with a mysterious aura.

The sound of Treena's shrill voice reeled Amanda back. "Oh, wow, I gotta get me one of these tuning tridents for singing class!"

Drake snapped his fingers. "Betcha if you put that crystal trident into the etched trident in the keystone, it acts like a key and unlocks those ancient secrets your Aunt Flo found out about. Maybe that's why she kept it hidden, so it wouldn't fall into the wrong hands. Maybe it's the key to *unlimited riches*." He rubbed his palms together. "Sweet!"

Melody reclaimed the crystal trident from Treena and nodded. "Yes, I thought that too, Drake. I was so excited when I found this that I couldn't wait until morning. So, I ran outside in my pajamas during the middle of the night to place it in the keystone."

"And?" Treena asked, biting her bottom lip.

"And...nothing. No big revelations, no psychic perceptions, no heart-stopping show." Melody blushed.

Drake frowned. He hiked up his baggy blue jeans, then pulled down his red T-shirt with the dragon on it, before he said, "Did you try reading out any of those riddles after you put the crystal trident in the keystone?"

"I tried nearly every riddle in the book until I got so frustrated I almost ripped the bloody pages out," Melody replied, still red-faced. She glanced at the trident and squeezed it. "Why on earth would my Aunt Florence bother to write down all those peculiar riddles if they had nothing to do with this thing? There has got to be some kind of connection between the riddles and this trident."

Drake puffed his cheeks. "Can I see the book, Melody?"

"Well, if anyone can figure out this gibberish it's you, Drake Bailey," Melody said. She dipped into the pocket of her long black skirt and pulled out a small tan book the width and length of her hand. She passed it to him.

"What's that gold design on the front cover?" Treena asked, peering over his shoulder.

"It's called the Eye of Horus," Drake explained, unlocking the clasp holding the book closed. "It's the ancient Egyptian symbol of protection." He moved a finger onto a page. "Here's what's written on May fourth, 1429—*The plowman's daughter has need of me, to take up arms and protect thee. To halt a madman's wild arrow, I must go to Orleans and protect the sparrow.*"

Treena scrunched her face. "Fortune cookie messages make more sense than that does."

"Gibberish," Drake grunted. He slammed the book shut.

Still feeling the funky effects from that strange resonance, Amanda slowly stood. Gaining her balance, she stepped out of the garden. *Book of riddles. Crystal trident. Stone arch. What's the connection?* She brushed dirt from her overalls. Nothing came to her. It was a blank page to this poet. And she hated blank pages.

"Hey, Amanda, I didn't see you there," Treena said, waving to her. Then she stopped. "What's with the Mother Earth look?"

Melody looked at Amanda. Her face fell. "Amanda, you've got dirt all over you. What happened?"

Drake laughed. "Looks like someone tackled *her* for a change!"

Amanda looked down. Her eyes widened. What had happened? Her head was buzzing, like she'd had one too many of those caffeine energy drinks. *Think, think, think.* But nothing came to her. It was as if her mind was in limbo. "I-I'm not sure. Don't remember. Must have tripped."

"Hold the presses!" Treena shouted, wide-eyed. "Drake, give Amanda the book of riddles."

"Why?" Drake asked.

"She's a poet. Ergo—she understands gibberish."

Melody sighed. "Perhaps a pair of fresh eyes would be of help, Drake."

"Fine. But if I can't figure it out, then I highly doubt a less than average student will."

Coming out of her fog, Amanda glared at Drake. "Poetry's my turf, not yours, brain-drain."

She strutted over to the end of the porch, snatched the book out of his hands, and stared at it. The book itself, not much bigger than her hand, had a thin black spine and the gold embossed Eye of Horus in the middle of its cover. A small copper clasp, now opened, wagged at her like a berating finger. Amanda turned the cover and saw an indentation in the shape and size of the crystal trident. She thumbed through the book's yellowed pages and noticed that each page was dated. However, the dates weren't in chronological order. Days, months, and years seem to skip from one century to another. And under each recorded date was a handwritten riddle like the one Drake had read. Amanda frowned. It was gibberish, all right. No limericks nor haikus here—just really bad poetry. Even she wrote better stuff than this.

"Boo!"

Amanda screamed. She dropped the book and twirled around. It was Ravi Sharma wearing his garden grubs—brown cargo pants and a worn navy sweatshirt. Ear buds were stuffed in both his ears. A wiggling movement above Ravi's brows held Amanda's attention, until she realized what it was—a grotesque green worm protruding from his forehead. It looked as if it had eaten its way out of Ravi's skull and was going in for seconds. He swayed his head from side to side for effect.

"You're one sick puppy, Sharma," she muttered.

"I always knew you had worms for brains, Ravi. This just confirms it!" Treena giggled, smacking her hand against her dark gray pants.

Ravi yanked his ear buds out and smirked. "You'd better be nice to me, Treena. I'm doing all the makeup for this year's spring play. One slip of the brush and presto, you'll have one eyebrow instead of two."

Treena folded her arms over her plum shirt. "Geez, since when did we change from performing *The Wizard of Oz* to doing the stage adaptation of *Zombieland?*"

Melody shook her head. "Do you two ever stop arguing?"

Drake snorted. "Is global warming fictional?" He jumped off the deck and snatched up the book before Amanda could.

"Hey, I wasn't finished with that!" she snapped.

"Melody figures I'm the only one smart enough to decipher the riddles in this book, so I'd say you're done," Drake replied over his shoulder, as he headed for the sanctuary of the tall, blooming lilac bush near the corner of the house.

Amanda's throat tightened. It was time to channel one of her warrior ancestors. She sprinted after Drake. "Give me that back, or I swear I'll—"

She never got a chance to finish. A tall man emerged from behind the bush and slammed into Drake before she reached him.

She watched helplessly as Drake rolled across the freshly cut grass. The book of riddles was knocked out of his hands. Amanda froze. Her stomach clenched. Now she remembered. Everything was clear. And it was too late to warn the others. Jordan's uncle, Professor John Lucas—a.k.a. Norman Bates—had arrived.

"Where is it, Jordan?" he shouted.

"Drake!" Melody yelled. She handed off the crystal trident to Treena and then hurtled over the porch railing.

Melody scooped up the nearest garden tool—a rake—and turned to face Jordan's uncle. She held it out in front of her, and yelled, "You beast, how dare you!"

The professor put up his hands, looked at Melody, and then looked down at Drake. "Huh? Oh sorry, kid, I didn't see you. Are you okay?"

All Drake did was nod. But Melody didn't appear to like his manners much. She poked him with the rake.

"Ouch! Hey, what was that for?" Professor Lucas asked, wincing.

"I don't like trespassers on my property, much less rude ones. Now leave before—"

"Before you decide to rake me over the coals?" he interrupted with a grin.

"Hey, buster, you're lucky Melody doesn't have a sword!" Treena heckled from the porch. "She's won three fencing titles in a row!"

"She's also the daughter of a knight, so she's got connections with the royal family, if you know what I mean." Ravi ran a finger under his throat.

Melody drew the rake back. Before she had a chance to assault him again, Jordan Jensen flew around the corner, frantically waving his arms. "Don't hit him, Melody. He's with me! He's my uncle!"

Melody growled, squeezed the rake's handle, then slowly dropped her shoulders, like a watchdog lowering its hackles. She tossed the rake aside and hurried over to Drake. She slipped a slim finger under his chin, and looked him over.

"Does it hurt anywhere, Drake?" she asked, moving his chin from side to side.

"The kid's fine, lady," Professor Lucas said, waving his hand. "No blood, no bruises, no broken bones. In my book, that means he'll survive."

Melody's beautiful green eyes changed like a forest on fire. She slowly guided Drake to a large glittering boulder and lowered him on it. Amanda heard Melody grunt.

"Uh-oh, Melody's about to go for that guy's jugular," Treena said, jumping down from the porch.

Melody whirled around, advanced toward the professor, and poked him in the chest. "And what book are you referring to—*A Simpleton's Guide to Raising Children?* Do you always stick that gigantic foot of yours in your mouth?"

He rubbed his chest, and then growled. "Look, lady…I'm here for one reason and one reason only!"

"Harassment? Intimidation? Child abuse? Well, which one is it?" Melody snapped, crossing her arms over her crisp white blouse.

"Here, Amanda, better take this," Treena said, passing her the crystal trident like a baton in a relay. She snapped her fingers at Ravi. "Come on, Sharma, time for damage control."

A fuzzy sensation came over Amanda the moment Treena handed her the crystal trident. The queasiness was back, but not so intense. Her senses started to go haywire as electrical currents surged through her body, making Amanda feel like she was trapped inside the Bermuda Triangle. She opened her mouth to yell for help, but no sound came out. She closed her eyes, and then opened them to look around. Everything around her appeared in slow motion. She saw Treena bound over to stand beside Melody and hook her arm inside of Melody's arm. Ravi joined Treena and grabbed Melody's other arm. Their voices sounded muffled, out of sync to her. They pulled; she pulled back. They pulled again, but Melody held firm. She wasn't going anywhere. Jordan jumped in and tried to referee his uncle away from Melody, but that didn't work either.

Drake was still on the boulder, his face buried in his palms, grass shavings all over his back. *Get the book,* a voice whispered in her ear. Startled, Amanda turned around. But no one was there.

"Get what book?" Amanda muttered, looking around until she spied the book of riddles Drake had snatched from her under a patch of blossoming tulips.

Amanda was there in seconds, as if she'd flown across the yard. Shaken, and not sure how she'd traveled there so fast, Amanda scooped up the book. The crystal trident accidently came in contact with the golden Eye of Horus on the cover, and like crossing hot wires, sparks flew out. A sudden jolt ran through her body. Her eyes widened. Her mind cleared. She knew what she had to do.

Moving as if she had wings on her feet, Amanda ran to the stone arch. She cast off her sandals, shoved the book of riddles down the bib of her overalls, and stuck her foot into one of the crevices in the arch. With one hand holding the crystal trident tight, she used her other to reach up to the next crevice and pull herself up toward the keystone. She repeated this once more, as if she was a skilled rock climber. Hugging the column tightly, Amanda leaned into the archway and stretched her arm enough to place the crystal trident inside the engraved trident in the keystone, as Melody told Drake and Treena she had done last night. It was a perfect fit. Amanda wiped her forehead and climbed down.

The trident acted like a magnet drawing the sun's rays into it, absorbing the heat offered. Amanda's ears started to ring at the high-pitched sound resonating from the crystal. It was an annoying tone—like the shrillness of an activated fire alarm. She winced, preferring the sullen beeps of her alarm clock, and wished she could hit the snooze button. Then, a burst of light shot out of the trident and covered Amanda where she stood, baptizing her in a brilliant flash. She fell to her knees and started to shake.

A light appeared from inside the stone arch. Amanda's mouth opened. The light was dim at first, and then it became brighter and brighter. The arguing behind her stopped. She attempted to stand, but stumbled. Drake caught her elbow in time. Her breathing was uneven, almost over-worked. She felt Drake gently squeeze her arm, and she jumped, as if she'd been jarred out of sleep. She hugged her body and took a deep breath.

"W-What's going on, Amanda?" Drake asked in a whisper.

Before she could answer him, she heard a *swoosh*, like someone had just opened an elevator door. A warm gentle breeze danced across her bronze skin, and she shivered. So did Drake. A high-pitched sound pulsed through them, and they took a few steps back.

Drake's eyes widened. "Do...do you see that, Amanda?"

Amanda didn't answer. She couldn't. She was too busy staring at the beautiful, radiant face within the archway. Melody's angel was back. Only this time, she wasn't singing.

7. The City of the Golden Gates

A shimmering ball of light from inside the archway shot out at them. Amanda lunged for her sandals, while Drake hauled her out of the light's path and dragged her back to join the others.

"W-What's happening?" Ravi asked, releasing his hold on Melody. He winced at the brightness.

"I-I'm not sure," Treena replied, as she let go of Melody's arm to hood her eyes.

Amanda looked around. Everyone seemed to be operating at normal speed now. Voices were distinguishable and she didn't feel queasy anymore. She noticed Professor Lucas was breathing wildly, as if he had asthma, staring spellbound into the archway.

"Uncle John? Are you okay?" Jordan asked. He smacked his uncle's back.

Professor Lucas shrugged him off, but remained silent as he continued to stare at the light. Jordan tugged on one of his uncle's sleeves. When that didn't work, Jordan did the next best thing. He slapped him across the face.

He flinched. "Ouch! What the hell was that for?"

Jordan raked his tawny hair. "Sorry. My bad. I thought you were freaking out on me."

"I-It's so beautiful," Melody whispered.

"Amazing," Professor Lucas muttered, getting his breathing under control.

"Do you know what it is, Uncle John?" Jordan asked.

"Not what. Who," Amanda replied, wiping her mouth.

Treena's jaw dropped and she stared at Amanda. So did Jordan.

"Has that light shrunk your brain cells, Sault?" he asked.

"Amanda's right," Drake added. "I saw her too—a woman's face in the archway."

Ravi snorted. "Did this floating face tell you what she wanted? Hey, I know, maybe she's looking for a body to snatch and brains to eat."

Drake wrung his hands. Amanda gently nudged him. "No, Drake, remember what you felt? There was nothing hostile about her."

"Really?" Treena blurted. She pointed to the book of riddles peeking out of Amanda's bib. "Here's a newsflash for you, Amanda, maybe she's looking for that book. Maybe you should give her what she wants."

Amanda shook her head. "She doesn't want the book."

Treena wrinkled her nose. "Details, please. What does she want?"

Amanda's whole body relaxed. "She wants *us.*"

As if on cue, the brilliant white light started to speed up and spread out like freshly spilled milk. Nobody moved. The light mimicked the sun by swallowing their shadows and caressing their bodies. It warmed Amanda through to her core, and from somewhere deep inside, she knew she could trust this light, this radiance. As the light continued to bathe them, an incredible pulling sensation—what she imagined a tractor beam from a sci-fi flick would feel like—fused with it. Like being on a moving walkway, there was nothing to fear as her body was gently drawn toward the glowing stone arch.

Amanda noticed Treena trying to brake with both feet, but she couldn't. She glanced down and jerked. Her mouth opened, but no words came out. Treena's feet weren't touching the ground. She was levitating. They all were. Whoever wanted them, wanted them bad.

"Whoa, we're floating!" Jordan blurted. "We gotta be a least two feet off the ground!"

Ravi grabbed Treena's arm. "Are you feeling what I'm feeling?"

Treena nodded. "I think so. I feel warm, light, and tingly, like a bubble in a tub."

They were within a few feet of the stone archway. Its mottled marble shone more brilliantly than before. Feeling calm and relaxed, Amanda gave in to a sigh. Nothing mattered. All her problems, any worries, seemed gone and solved.

"Hey, my cell phone won't work," Ravi said. "I'm not getting any signal."

"You're right, Ravi," Treena said. "No bars on mine, either."

"Crap, my cell's not receiving anything," Jordan added, holding it up.

"Maybe the white light is full of radiation particles that are interfering with the cell tower's frequency," Drake said.

"Great," Treena muttered, stuffing her cell phone into her pocket. "How's my drama coach supposed to get ahold of me?"

"I-I-I think you're gonna have plenty of drama to deal with any second," Ravi stammered.

They were almost inside the glowing archway. Its light felt warm and welcoming, like the rising summer sun. Treena stuck her thumbs in the straps of her khaki backpack as if it doubled as a magic parachute. Amanda mimicked Treena and grasped the straps on Jordan's backpack that she was still wearing. Ravi was the only other person wearing one, so all the rest had nothing to break their fall if that light suddenly cut them loose.

The brilliant, fathomless glow swallowed Amanda, blinding her. Calm and silence overrode her senses. In that moment, two things happened—Amanda sensed that there was no separation between her and the others—as if they were all connected by these tiny threads of light. Second, she started to feel as though she were free falling, moving fast and out of control. She regained her vision, just as the white light exploded into a whirling rainbow.

Drake laughed. "Wicked! This feels like a ride at Disneyland!"

"It feels better than that!" Jordan replied. "I've been to Disneyland twice, and there's no ride that even comes close to this!"

"It's as if we can fly!" Treena shouted, doing a somersault in mid-air.

"It does feel wonderful, doesn't it?" Melody said dreamily. Amanda grabbed both ankles and flipped herself over. She giggled. This freedom, this feeling, this flux was awesome. The huge, spiraling rainbow surrounding the group of seven gently juggled them in mid-air like floating balls in a never-ending lottery game. She glanced over at Jordan's uncle. His cheeks were sucked in, and his body flopped one way then another like a fish out of water.

"Is your uncle okay, Jordan?" she asked.

Jordan maneuvered over to his uncle by spreading his arms and legs wide as if he were a free-falling parachutist. He grasped his uncle's shoulder and shook him. "Uncle John? Uncle John! Don't make me slap you again!"

He reached over, grabbed Jordan, and kissed him on the forehead. "It's all true, Jordan! It's all true!"

Jordan squirmed. "What's true?"

"Time *flows* through us," he answered, his voice cracking as if he were a young boy again.

The whirling rainbow burst into shards of light, and they all touched bottom.

It felt soft—like a cushy trampoline—as Amanda, her classmates, Melody, and Professor Lucas bounced easily until they all stood still. Then the ground became solid again. Polished marble walls and finely crafted pillars materialized through the fading light. A sudden high-pitched buzzing noise made her wince. Everyone seemed to hear it too; they cringed in unison. The sound of waves crashing against a shore replaced the buzzing, and a set of deep purple curtains miraculously appeared in front of them. Amanda rubbed her eyes. In the time it took her to take a breath, the curtains were drawn. The brilliant white light that had pulled them into the stone arch now hovered between the open curtains. It started to radiate out, then draw in, out, then in, changing its shape with each rhythmic movement, until it finally transformed into a woman.

The woman was beautiful in an otherworldly way. She had long, fair, flowing hair adorned with quartz crystals. Piercing blue eyes stared back at Amanda like she was peering into her soul. She had a long narrow face with high cheek bones that tapered down to a firm chin. Her nose was long and slender. Amanda smiled at her. The woman smiled back. Her teeth were white, small, and even. She was perfect in every way. A rich-blue sleeveless linen robe adorned her slim body, accentuating her ivory skin.

I wonder if she's a princess. Amanda didn't doubt it, especially with all the jewelry the woman wore. A sparkling metallic snake bracelet wound around her left arm, a string of gleaming pearls and shells hung around her neck, and a silver belt strewn with various green, blue, and red gems hugged her waist. The only piece of clothing that didn't seem to belong was a plain pair of woven sandals.

Melody pushed Drake behind her and took a few steps forward. "I demand that you tell us where we are!"

The beautiful woman gave Melody a gentle smile, and nodded. She opened her arms wide and said, "Welcome to the Temple of Poseidon, in the City of the Golden Gates."

Melody jerked. "I-I beg your pardon?"

"Atlantis," Professor Lucas answered in a whisper. "We're in Atlantis."

8. The Code of Time

"Not quite Atlantis, Professor Lucas. Only what is left of it."

"Hey, how did you know my uncle's name?" Jordan asked.

The woman smiled. "I know much, Jordan Jensen. All of your names are only a sampling."

"A-Are we dead?" Ravi asked, rubbing his prosthesis.

The woman laughed; to Amanda it sounded like she hadn't laughed in a long time. The enchanting sound made Amanda's skin ripple, as if a hundred feathers caressed the inside of her body.

Melody lightly squeezed Ravi's shoulder. "I don't see what's so funny. Are we dead or not?" she asked directly.

"Oh, no, Melody Spencer, you are all alive and well. I was laughing at the wiggling worm on Ravi Sharma's forehead."

Ravi's eyes widened. He quickly yanked the rubber worm off his head. Treena snickered, so he turned and whipped it at her. He missed. His shoulders sagged.

"Fear not, Ravi Sharma," the mysterious woman said. "In my time, mask-makers were revered for their talents. You must realize that what has been taken from you in life has been transformed and given back to you in many different ways. Your imagination, for example, has become more expressive, more alive than before your accident, through the many masks you create. Well done."

Ravi straightened his body, and the hard lines on his face disappeared. "How do you know this? Who are you?"

She started to walk toward him. "My name is Lilith. I am the Fiftieth Magus of the Arcane Tradition and the guardian of the seventh Arch of Atlantis."

Silence echoed throughout the Temple of Poseidon. It didn't last long though, as Drake snorted. "Yeah right, and I'm one of the Knights of the Round Table."

Treena giggled. "Yeah, he's the one called Sir Douche-a-lot!"

Drake glared at Treena and then crossed his arms over his chest. Amanda guessed that if Drake had a tail, he'd be tucking it up his butt.

A shrill whistle sounded from behind Amanda. It was Professor Lucas. "Is that who I think it is?" he asked, pointing past the long, purple curtains.

Amanda searched for what the professor was talking about. When she saw it, her mouth fell open, and a deep breath followed. A gigantic golden statue—about half the size of the Statue of Liberty—was set in the middle of an opulent room. It was a bearded man wrapped in a bed sheet and standing in a chariot pulled by six winged horses. The twinkling chariot was circled by hundreds of small freaky-looking mermaids riding on dolphins. Ivory walls decorated with gold, silver, and another metal that sparkled like fire glittered back at Amanda. She blinked at the brilliance.

"Yes, Professor Lucas, it is Poseidon, the father of Atlantis."

Professor Lucas strode past Ravi and Jordan, tousling the boy's hair in excitement. "Yes! My research wasn't bunk after all! It was fact!"

"What research, Uncle John?" Jordan asked.

"The research I've been working on most of my life—to prove Atlantis did exist," Professor Lucas replied. "That this ancient civilization wasn't a legend or myth, but an actual place." He removed his silly-looking fishing hat, reached in, pulled out a small photograph, and passed it around. Amanda's eyes bugged. It was a picture of the same arch in Melody's garden.

"You see—" the professor continued, shoving his hat back on "—during a recent dig in Guatemala with some co-workers, I found this arch, which looks exactly like the one we were transported through. As I started to interpret the engraved hieroglyphics and alchemical symbols on it, I *knew* it had to have come from Atlantis, but had a hard time convincing anyone. It was only when I translated the words, *Time flows through us,* engraved in the keystone, that I realized that this was the secret code of nature. So I started paying close attention to the repeating patterns inscribed on the arch. The Atlanteans knew that if they paid attention to the subtle patterns in nature they could learn to harness this energy and flow with it. And since time is a form of energy, I deduced that what we unearthed was a type of teleportation portal—a device that would allow us to flow with time."

"Yes," Lilith said. "Professor Lucas broke the code."

Amanda noticed a change in Lilith's voice—it had gotten lower—and her face had turned sad. Lilith bent her head like a branch about to break.

"What code?" Melody asked as she handed the professor back his photo.

Lilith forced a half-smile. "The code of time."

"Wait, I don't get it," Amanda said. "If this *is* Atlantis—or what's left of it—how come you're still alive? I mean, that would make you around twelve thousand years old."

Treena scratched her nose with her thumb. "I dunno, Amanda, Lilith doesn't look a day over six thousand years to me."

Lilith smiled fully. "I exist in the *element* of time, Amanda Sault. My consciousness, my memory, is locked into the Arch of Atlantis where I survive through the energy of the spirals."

"What do spirals have to do with time?" Ravi asked.

"Plenty, Ravi," Professor Lucas said excitedly. "Spirals are cyclic in nature. The Mayans knew this, and because they were such great astronomers, they understood that the cycles and rhythms in the sky correlated with everything here—"

Ravi's eyes glazed over. His cheek twitched twice before he held up his hand. "What was that middle thing again?"

Amanda rolled her eyes. "Allow me to translate. My grandmother told me that spirals exist in *everything.* In nature. In the sky. In the water. Even in our bodies. So in a way, we're all programmed by nature, and we're all connected. Spirals help us understand movement through the cycles of nature and passage of time. You know, like day changes into night, new moon into full moon, spring into summer, stuff like that."

"Amanda's got a point," Drake added. "Spirals exist in our DNA and fingerprints—our whole genetic makeup is based on spirals."

"Okay, that sort of makes sense, Amanda," Jordan said, "but what doesn't is how someone like *you* figured out the code of time." He shook his head. "My uncle's a professor, and it obviously took him years to crack it."

Amanda balled her fists. "Well, maybe I'm some kind of genius when it comes to cracking codes, *Jockstrap.*"

Ravi stifled a laugh.

"But, Amanda, Jordan has a point," Treena said. "How'd *you* figure out the code?"

Amanda felt her cheeks burn. She unclenched her hands and shrugged. "I dunno. The crystal trident…it did something to me. I-I guess I was just acting on a *feeling.*"

Amanda fell silent. Her body hardened, and her throat tightened. She became a statue, cast her eyes down, and stared at her feet.

"And it was a *good* feeling to act on, Amanda Sault," Lilith answered, as if coming alive again. "It was your cellular frequency that caused the crystal trident to resurrect itself. You broke the code by *natural* means, by tuning in, by *knowing* that through the power of the sun, the crystal trident would draw enough energy to activate the Arch of Atlantis. Well done."

Drake scrunched his face. "Okay, so what you're saying is that because the cells in Amanda's body are vibrating at the same speed and intensity as the crystal trident, she was able to use it to hook up to the sun's energy, and jumpstart the arch as if she were boosting a car battery?"

Lilith smiled. "Precisely, Drake Bailey."

"I…I have a frequency?" Amanda asked, breaking her vigilant stance.

"Un-uh, you got *cellular frequency*. You go, girl!" Treena clapped.

"You all have frequencies, Treena Mui, vibrating at different speeds and different levels," Lilith explained.

Treena beamed. "What speed am I?"

"Slow as snot," Ravi said.

Jordan and Drake laughed and high-fived Ravi.

"That's quite enough, boys," Melody said. "I'm sure Treena's frequency is adequate, as are all of ours, seeing as we're standing in the Temple of Poseidon. What I want to know is why we've been summoned—if that's the correct word—here?"

"Fair enough, Melody Spencer," Lilith said. "I shall do my best to answer you."

Lilith walked closer to them, as if bridging an invisible gap. Her magnificent blue robe brushed against Ravi's left hand, and he shuddered. He reached out to touch it again, but Lilith intercepted his hand and gave it a gentle squeeze. Then, she reached for Ravi's prosthesis, pried open the stiff fingers, and kissed his palm as if he were a long lost prince who had returned home. Ravi squeaked.

The lines of sadness returned to Lilith's face. "I miss children. There is something about them that is pure and good. They are always curious, always playful, and always forthright. Children are the keys to our future. And now, children are the only hope for our past."

"Hope for our past? What do you mean?" Ravi asked softly.

Lilith's smile returned. "There has been a terrible disruption in the timeline continuum, causing the code of time to be compromised. The seal to the door where evil dwells has been broken, releasing an unpredictable dark force—the same dark force responsible for the destruction of Atlantis—into the Earth's energy field. That is the reason why you are all here. To restore order to what has been disturbed. Or what will be. To maintain balance, and make sure changes do not occur in the past that will disrupt the future, for there is only one *true* history."

Melody pursed her lips. "Could you please be a little more specific?"

Lilith let go of Ravi's hand and grasped Melody by the shoulders. She slid her hands down the length of Melody's arms until their hands met. Melody shivered.

"Then, allow me to clarify, Melody Spencer. Recently, Professor Lucas broke the code held within the fifth Arch of Atlantis he found buried in a hidden section of Mayan ruins."

"Fifth? You mean there are more than two stone arches?" Professor Lucas asked in astonishment. He stared at his photograph.

Lilith nodded. "There were seven arches in total, and all are energetically connected to one another. That is why seven spirals are carved into the top of each arch. It is presumed that the first, second, third, fourth, and sixth were all destroyed with the final destruction of Atlantis, since they have never been activated. Only two arches remain: the fifth—the arch Professor Lucas discovered, and the seventh—the arch that brought you all here. The seventh was secretly moved to Egypt before Atlantis sank into the ocean, and it was eventually stored inside a secret chamber of the Great Pyramid. Originally, all the arches were created by a moral and virtuous group who called themselves the Children of the Law of One, to educate, reflect the truth, and preserve our knowledge." Lilith closed her eyes for a meditative moment, and then opened them. "It was a way of keeping the old red land alive throughout time."

"The old red land?" Melody asked. "Why does that sound so familiar?"

"Doncha remember, Melody?" Drake said. "I translated a line of glyphs that said the old red land, but couldn't figure out what that meant." His shoulders drooped.

Lilith released Melody. She reached out and smoothed her palm over Drake's close-shaven head. "Do not be too hard on yourself, Drake Bailey. Only those who were the descendants of Atlanteans used that term."

"If you're the guardian of the seventh Arch of Atlantis, then who's in charge of the fifth?" Jordan asked.

Lilith's face pinched like she was in pain. "The fifth arch was stolen after the first major earthquake, one hundred years before water and fire consumed Atlantis. An evil and selfish magus named Belial rebelled against the Children of the Law of One, and took the arch to a place now known as Central America. There he used the magic through the arch to control and enslave the people who lived there at the time. He became a powerful and corrupt leader. Those who defied him were killed or sacrificed. Fear and pain became a part of their lives. The original crystal trident was replaced by a terrible dark one. This black trident became the key to a world where only the Sons of Belial dwell. A place I think of as the *true* hell."

"Does Belial exist in the element of time too?" Treena asked.

"Belial exists in the blackest shadows of time, Treena Mui. A dark mind that lives in the past to feed off the evil energy continuing to stagnate there."

"Eww, it sounds like something a vampire would do," Amanda said.

Lilith nodded. "Yes, it does. However, the true essence of Belial—the wickedest part of him—has been dormant for centuries, imprisoned inside the fifth arch by a powerful leader named Kukulkan. Now everything has changed because this dark, evil power has been released back into the world by a corrupt man named Marcus Crowley."

Professor Lucas went rigid. His face turned ash white. "Crowley? That...that son-of-a-snake!"

"Do you know this man, Professor?" Melody asked.

"Yeah, my uncle knows him, Melody," Jordan said. "That loser set up Uncle John good so he could skip off with the treasure they found."

"Treasure?" Treena said skeptically. "Come on, Jordan, it's not like the arch is made of gold or silver. It's just a slab of old stone."

"Time is the ultimate treasure, Treena Mui," Lilith replied. "Think of what you could do if you went back into the past and changed whatever you wanted to. Certain lives could be saved and many criminals caught. You would know where treasures are buried and when disaster would strike. You could observe history firsthand, find the truth, and expel the lies. Think of what could be possible."

"Are you saying this douche-bag Crowley is gonna change the past, Lilith?" Amanda asked.

"And," Melody added quickly, "are you telling us that both the remaining arches are some sort of time portals? Do you have any idea how impossible that sounds?"

Lilith nodded. "It does sound impossible, but I assure you it is not, Melody Spencer. Marcus Crowley will change history if given the chance, and will do whatever Belial wants." Then as if Lilith had been magically recharged, she smiled and said, "But this will not happen because destiny has brought all seven of you here to become the *one* thing Belial fears the most."

Ravi inclined his head. "And what's that?"

"Timekeepers," Lilith answered. Her smile increased. "The Last Timekeepers."

9. *The Last Timekeepers*

Was this lady ready for the loony bin? Amanda's heart raced, trying to keep up with everything she'd downloaded so far. Atlantis—Lilith—time portal—cellular frequency—Belial—fear—Timekeepers—correction, the Last Timekeepers. She may be vibrating at a high velocity, but her brain certainly wasn't.

Amanda sighed. It was time to bring herself up to speed. "Okay, Lilith, suppose time travel is possible. What does a Timekeeper do and why is this Belial freak so afraid of them?"

"Timekeepers are the legendary guardians of history, Amanda Sault," Lilith said, smiling at her. "All Timekeepers are hand picked by destiny and sent into the past to keep time flowing naturally and on its proper course. Belial knows this and can do nothing to stop it. So he tempts those who choose to take the easier path to their deepest wants and desires. Belial truly becomes their shadow, always there, always lurking."

"So how come you called us the Last Timekeepers?" Amanda asked. "It sounds kind of final, like a death sentence."

Ravi groaned. "And what happened to the First Timekeepers?"

"All in good time, Ravi Sharma," Lilith replied. "And I assure you, Amanda Sault, it is anything but terminal. You are the Last Timekeepers because you are Earth's last chance to restore the balance in the time period Belial chooses to invade. Like the spirals teach, everything is interconnected, including time. It is important to understand that you are all to be a part of the greater good in order to secure hope for a new tomorrow, a new Earth."

"Great. No pressure there," Treena said.

"Belial has an easier time seeping into the minds of adults than children." Lilith swept her eyes over them. "He is the shadow side of humanity—the voice of knowledge, of suffering, of lies—yet it is children who call his bluff. Although you are not completely immune to his evil whisperings, you are more aware, more awake."

"This Belial loser sounds an awful lot like the devil," Drake said.

"He is the darkest part of ourselves and knows it. Belial taps into people's anger, hatred, and fears. This is what he did with Professor Crowley. Like Amanda Sault, his cellular frequency was an exact match to the black crystal trident he found hidden in a secret compartment located in the top portion of the fifth arch."

"Damn, I shouldn't have trusted Crowley!" Professor Lucas yelled, smacking his thighs. "I knew that snake was asking too many questions and sniffing around my research material way too much. I should have paid more attention. I'm such an idiot!"

"You'll get no argument from me, Professor Lucas," Melody retorted. "And if any harm comes to the children, then so help me God, I'll—"

"Look, lady, I'm sorry you and the kids were dragged here too. If it makes you feel any better, then I'll be the Timekeeper and you and the kids can take that whirling rainbow bus back home."

"I'm afraid that will not be possible, Professor Lucas," Lilith replied. She swept a hand over Amanda and her classmates. "These children and Melody Spencer are as much Timekeepers as you are. Fate has brought you all here to work together as one. It was not your fault that Professor Marcus Crowley chose to explore the voice of evil—It was his. You can not blame yourself for the choices other people make; it is part of their journey, not yours. You must remember to stay true to yourself, Professor Lucas, and be as authentic as possible."

"But these are children you're talking about, Lilith," Melody said. "Surely you can't expect them to fight against the mind of the devil? That's crazy, and I forbid it!"

Lilith calmly met Melody's fiery green eyes. "Trust in what has been presented to you, Melody Spencer. I know you have known pain and sadness in your life, but you must understand that it is from these trials that you have learned so much about yourself, and grown even more."

Melody jerked sharply. "What the bloody hell are you talking about?"

"The loss of your own child has made you heartsick and over-protective." Lilith sighed. "Yet it has also created a healer and nurturer who helps others adjust. It is a great gift."

Melody's mouth fell open. So did everyone else's. Melody had never mentioned anything about ever having kids or being married. Even in the hallways and walls of her house, there weren't any family photographs or portraits hanging to attest to her past. Only a few simple oil paintings of landscapes and fruit graced the walls. They were colorful, yet lifeless.

"How come you know so much about us, Lilith?" Drake asked. "Are you telepathic?"

Lilith ran a long, slender finger down the length of his nose. "Just as Belial seeks to take energy from your darkest thoughts, I search for your brilliance. This serves me best. I look for your strengths, dreams, and talents through your memories. It is a pity that most people do not do this because the world would be a happier and more balanced place to live."

Amanda smiled. That was what Grandmother Sault would have said. Happiness and balance made for a better world. Her grandmother and Lilith would have been BFFs for sure. Suddenly, Amanda's nose twitched. Crap, even in Atlantis she couldn't escape the wrath of pollen. She sneezed, and sneezed again. The book of riddles flew out of her overalls bib and landed in front of Professor Lucas.

"*Gesundheit*," Professor Lucas said. He grunted to pick it up. Amanda winced, hearing his knees crack. "What's this?" he asked, looking over the cover.

"It's a book of riddles Melody found with the crystal trident," Amanda replied. "I was just keeping it safe for her. You can pass it back to Melody."

"No, Professor Lucas. This book rightfully belongs to Amanda Sault," Lilith said, procuring the book from him. The professor frowned, looked down at his empty hands, and grunted. Lilith looked at Amanda approvingly and handed it to her. "The Timekeepers' log has chosen *you* to be the Scribe."

Dumbfounded, Amanda stared at the book of riddles—now dubbed the Timekeepers' log—in her hands. Before Amanda could ask what she had meant, Lilith bowed regally, turned around, and started walking toward the huge golden statue of Poseidon.

"What's a Scribe?" Treena asked.

"Isn't that like some kind of writer, only more disciplined?" Jordan guessed.

Ravi chuckled. "Well if it is, then Amanda's the wrong person to be a Scribe!"

Amanda didn't hesitate. She poked Ravi in the ribs with the book.

"Amanda can write!" Treena blurted. "FYI—she had a poem published in the *White Pines Weekly* last month."

Amanda's cheeks were blazing now. It was a good thing that her skin was bronze—it hid most of her blush. She had handed in her poem under a pseudonym. It had been their secret.. Amanda caught Jordan flashing an incisor like a shark.

He snickered. "Hey, guys, imagine that, a tomboy poet. Roses are red. Violets are blue. I get sore knees—when I tackle you!"

The boys broke out in laughter. The girls did not.

"This is ridiculous!" Melody burst out, pushing back tendrils of dark hair out of her face. "You children can barely get along with one another. How on earth are you possibly going to work together as Timekeepers when your lives may depend on it?"

Amanda stared at the Timekeepers' log. Melody had a point. Even in class, their seats were far apart from each other. Maybe this Timekeeper thing wasn't such a good idea. Amanda clutched the log to her chest and glanced down at the reflective marble tiles. How could she manage the job of Scribe when she had enough on her plate with an assignment on "The Chivalry of Knights" due Monday? Amanda lifted her head. She jumped, shocked to find Lilith standing in front of her. In Lilith's hands dangled seven strange-looking necklaces made of a metal that sparkled like embers in a campfire. Attached on the end of each necklace was a light blue stone, the size of a walnut.

Lilith smiled as she gently placed one of the necklaces around Amanda's neck. "Here, you will have need of this, Amanda Sault."

Amanda accepted it with a smile and looked it over as Lilith doled out the rest of the necklaces to the others. It wasn't as heavy as she thought it would be; in fact it was about half the weight of a cell phone. The blue stone was set in place by thin pieces of flickering metal. She didn't think it was gold; it appeared smooth and shiny, closer to the color of copper. Amanda felt her palm heat up before she reached for the clear, blue stone. It cooled her palm instantly, as if she had submerged her hand into a deep, glacier lake.

"Uh, don't take this the wrong way, but jewelry isn't my style," Drake said, as he tried to dodge Lilith. "But, if you've got any solid gold skateboards, I'll take one of those!"

"Ditto!" Ravi added.

"You will need this if you are to be a Timekeeper, Drake Bailey. It is called a Babel necklace. It will break any language barriers that you may come across."

"Language barriers?" Treena asked, rolling the blue stone between her palms. "What do you mean?"

"Different cultures speak in different tongues, Treena Mui," Lilith explained. "The Babel necklace is attuned to all languages here on Earth, extinct or existing. It will act as a receiver as well as a transmitter. In other words, you will be able to understand everyone you meet, and they in turn, will understand what you say to them."

Drake looked doubtful, but he put the necklace on.

"Sweet! I can hardly wait to try this out in French class!" Jordan said.

Lilith pursed her full lips and shook her head firmly. "The Babel necklace only works when you are on a Timekeeper mission, Jordan Jensen."

"What's this necklace made of, Lilith?" Professor Lucas asked. "I've never quite seen a metal like this before. It's shinier than gold."

"It's orichalcum, Professor Lucas. You can't find it anywhere else but on Atlantis. The blue stone is a special crystal that has been energized by the sun for at least a hundred years."

"Excuse me, Lilith," Ravi cut in. "How long does a Timekeeper mission last?"

Lilith shrugged. "It takes as long as it takes, Ravi Sharma. Some Timekeeper missions take a few hours or a day to complete. Others may take weeks or even months to accomplish."

Lilith said it like it was no big deal. *Weeks? Months? Won't we be missed?* Amanda's mind went to amber alert, and she shook her head. "Lilith, we can't be gone for that long. Our faces and names would be plastered all over police bulletin boards, milk cartons, and probably on television."

Treena jumped. "OMG! Television? Really? I hope my parents use one of my head shots from my portfolio!"

"You'd be dangerous if you had a brain, Treena," Jordan said. "Amanda's being serious."

"You don't know what serious is, Jordan!" Ravi growled. "If I'm not back home by tonight, then the battery in my my electric hand won't get recharged. And if it doesn't get recharged, I can't use it! And if I can't use it, then I can't punch your freaking brains out!"

Both Amanda and Jordan took a few steps back. But Lilith held her ground, grasped Ravi by the chin, and said, "Trust, Ravi Sharma. You must learn this. All will be provided for you and the others. You have what you need with you, as well as the *unseen power* inside of you, to face each obstacle you meet. Everyone does. Now here, Ravi Sharma, I have another gift."

Ravi seemed on the verge of tears as Lilith rolled up his right arm's sleeve. Amanda had never seen Ravi's entire artificial hand, only the part he allowed the world to see. She had never touched it, but heard it thud against his desk enough times to know it was made of hard plastic. The color was a close match to Ravi's light brown skin, and it appeared to end about four inches away from his pink-scarred elbow. Amanda and the others watched in silence as Lilith flipped over Ravi's prosthesis and removed the attached battery. She then replaced it with a long, narrow purple crystal surrounded by tiny strips of that orichalcum stuff. It clicked in perfectly, as if it was made for that purpose.

"What did you give him?" Melody asked, moving in for a closer look.

Lilith rolled down Ravi's sleeve and let go of his arm. "A piece of Atlantean know-how. Go ahead and give it a try, Ravi Sharma."

Ravi wiped away the glisten from his eyes and nodded. He opened and closed his prosthesis with ease, just as he could always do. His stony facial expression changing into one of awe. A light had clicked on for Ravi the moment his fingers began to move in unison, synchronizing with each other, going back and forth with a rhythm of their own. Amanda found herself mirroring Ravi's movements with her hand. Finally, he moved his thumb down, then up, as tears flooded his eyes.

"I-I can *feel* my hand as…as if it were real again," Ravi choked.

Then, Ravi wiped his face and flashed Lilith the thumbs up sign.

Lilith returned his gesture and said, "Like the Babel necklace, this crystal battery only operates when you're on a Timekeeper mission, Ravi Sharma."

"Well, you've solved Ravi's problem, Lilith," Drake said, "but *what if* a Timekeeper mission lasts more than a few hours?"

"Time is an illusion, Drake Bailey," Lilith answered calmly. "You can never 'measure' it. Time exists simultaneously. Therefore you and the other Timekeepers will never be missed and will never age during the entire stay of each Timekeeper mission."

"But, Lilith, how do we know what part of history we're supposed to keep from changing?" Jordan asked.

"That is the Scribe's job, Jordan Jensen," Lilith replied. Then she held out her hand to Amanda. "Here, this is for you, Amanda Sault. Every Scribe needs one."

A thin, long, clear crystal glittered in Lilith's open hand. It was about the shape and size of a pen. A dark blue point glowed at one end. Amanda picked it up and let her thumb slide down the length of it.

"Thanks, Lilith. Um, what exactly is this thing?"

"It is your crystal chalkis, Amanda Sault. You use it to record each Timekeeper mission."

"But how do I know what the mission will be?" Amanda asked.

"The crystal chalkis will tell you in the same way it told Frances Tarbush and later, Florence Whitney. Just trust the voice that comes into your head, and transcribe what you hear into the Timekeepers' log."

"M-My great aunt was a Timekeeper?" Melody asked, covering her mouth.

"Yes, Melody Spencer. Both Florence Whitney and Frances Tarbush were wonderful Timekeepers. They learned how to flow with time and not be trapped by it. Unfortunately, Max Tarbush chose to take another path and was not so lucky."

"Wait a minute. Max Tarbush? Why does that name ring a bell?" Professor Lucas asked, as he pushed his fishing hat off his forehead to scratch it. He snapped his fingers. "Oh, yeah, now I remember, he was presumed murdered sometime back in the early twentieth century. The urban legend goes that Tarbush got into some money problems with a few of the lumber mills in White Pines. Apparently the man loved to gamble. Then one night while closing up his hotel for the evening, Tarbush was attacked. The rumors say it was probably someone Tarbush cheated on in a card game. A few of the hotel's guests heard shouting going on downstairs, and by the time they went to investigate, they found a puddle of blood in the backyard, but no trail. Now, this is where the mystery comes in, because a severed hand was also discovered on the ground, still twitching. To this day, Tarbush's body has never materialized."

"Cool story, Professor Lucas. Sounds like a mob hit to me," Treena said, running a finger underneath her throat.

"On the contrary, Treena Mui," Lilith said. "Max Tarbush disappeared into time."

"Disappeared into time? How?" Ravi asked, his voice almost squeaking.

"Max Tarbush was a victim of his own dark machinations, Ravi Sharma," Lilith answered. She turned and glided toward a marble column.

Amanda noticed that the top of the tall, polished column was covered by a shimmering, purple cloth. Lilith lifted the cloth to reveal a crystal ball the size of a huge grapefruit, held up by two bronze hands.

Lilith stepped back. "It would be easier if I *show* you what happened. All you need to do is take a deep breath and stare into Poseidon's Eye."

Amanda inhaled, and suddenly she was drifting, as if she were being hypnotized, sliding, whirling, and spiraling into another dimension, another place. When Amanda's head stopped spinning, she saw a young girl wearing a ratty apron-like dress. The girl was thin and had dark iridescent hair tied in a neat bun. She was serving drinks to a group of men playing cards at a table in a parlor decorated with ugly floral wallpaper. Amanda started to make out voices—the men sounded drunk, loud, and obnoxious. A man with dark bushy hair and an equally dark bushy mustache, dressed in a pin-striped suit, stood up and pointed toward a large, picturesque window.

"I'll wager that stone arch to clear all my debts with you," the man said.

Amanda looked at what he was pointing to, and her eyes bugged. It was the Arch of Atlantis! The young girl dropped the tray of drinks. "Oh no, you mustn't, sir! Mrs. Tarbush would be most upset!"

Another man, wearing a cleaner, pressed suit, laughed. "I see the women have the run of your establishment, Max. It's no wonder your finances are in such a mess!"

Knowing now it was Max Tarbush, Amanda watched him grab the girl's arm and twist it viciously. "Hold your tongue, Florence! Else you'll be in for the beating of your life!"

"B-B-But, sir, Mrs. Tarbush adores that stone arch! I shall tell her, I will!"

Max Tarbush raised his hand and started to hit Florence, over and over again. She screamed, but no one came to help her. The other men got up and left. Blood drizzled from Florence's face and speckled her apron. Amanda's heart raced, her fists balled, her mouth turned to cotton. Then, as if time shifted, she saw young Florence curled up next to a weathered shed. The night sky rumbled and flickered until a flash of forked lightning made Amanda flinch. A stout woman with short brown hair suddenly appeared in the garden, holding out a lantern as if searching for someone. She wore pleated pants and a blouse with ruffles. A Babel necklace swung across her ample chest. A sudden gasp escaped her broad lips upon finding the beaten girl, and she collapsed next to her. Placing the lantern on the ground, she ran her ruddy hands gently along the length of Florence's thin body until she cupped her swollen and bruised face.

"Did...did Maxwell do this, child?" the woman asked in horror.

Florence whimpered. "Aye, Mrs. Tarbush, but I stood up to him. He was going to wager your beautiful stone arch in a card game while you were away. But I told him he mustn't. I knew everything would change if he did."

Amanda could feel the woman's anger rippling under her own skin. Raging against the man—her husband, Max Tarbush—Frances Tarbush stood, and spying an axe leaning against the shed, she grabbed it. It didn't take her long to find Max, who was sitting alone at the same card table, pouring himself another drink. Amanda's nostrils flared. The heavy scent of cheap whiskey filled her up, made her retch.

"How dare you lay a beating on that girl!" Frances seethed. "And how many times have I told you, the stone arch is off limits to you, Maxwell!"

Max looked up from his stupor and laughed. Amanda could tell that Frances was at her limit by the way she gripped the axe handle. Then, hearing nothing but glass shattering, Amanda winced as Frances swept the axe across the table, grazing her husband's forehead, and knocking him off his chair. He screamed, clutching his head.

With the axe still in her grasp, Frances bolted out the door, into the backyard, and headed for the Arch of Atlantis. Not far behind, Max stumbled and staggered across the ground, spewing obscenities Amanda had never heard before, but that brought a blush to her cheeks.

A bolt of lightning ripped through the darkness and hit the crystal trident set in the keystone of the Arch of Atlantis. Finger-like sparks flew from the trident, and the arch started to hum. The sound ripped through Amanda's body, making her feel woozy, almost to the point of being sick. Frances led her husband to the threshold of the droning arch, and turned, holding the axe out in front of her.

Max skidded to a stop, almost falling. His forehead was cut and bleeding, his breathing irregular and harsh. He wiped his brow and held out his hand. "Give me the axe, Frances, and I'll spare the girl's life."

Frances shook her head and stood her ground. Amanda swallowed hard, tasting bile, just as Max charged his wife. She stepped to the right, and Max went sailing into the archway, disappearing into a swirling black hole. Fear, anger, pain exploded through Amanda. She hugged herself. A morbid scream echoed out of the archway with such intensity, it knocked Frances off balance. She fell to the ground, and the axe flew out of her hands.

"Not so fast, my love!" Max sputtered as half his body emerged from the archway. He grabbed her foot. "I'll show you who wears the pants around here!"

Amanda jumped. His voice sounded mechanical. Part of him was still stuck in the dark, whirling void. Her eyes widened. He was planning to take his wife with him!

"Noooo!" Florence screamed and scrambled across the grass toward the axe.

Florence clenched her jaw and gripped the axe handle as if it were part of her. She raised the axe as far above her head as she could muster and then swung it down with enough force to chop off Max's hand. His screams permeated Amanda's being as she watched his blood gush everywhere. Suddenly, the arch released the crystal trident from its keystone just as the raging black whirlwind sucked Max into oblivion, leaving Frances and Florence behind, hugging each other in sudden silence.

Amanda shuddered, feeling the darkest part of humanity, of herself, leave her body in that instant. She knew it was there, yet she knew she was safe from all the Max Tarbushes in the world. Then it was over just as quickly as it had begun, and Amanda slipped back into the present.

Lilith carefully covered Poseidon's Eye with the purple cloth. "You must remember to make sure you protect those people living in the present by taking the crystal trident out of the keystone during each Timekeeper mission. It is imperative that you do this."

"Awesome, Lilith! That was better than any horror flick I've ever seen," Ravi said, rubbing his prosthesis. "It was like watching a totally hyped-up 3D version."

"How did Frances Tarbush find the crystal trident, Lilith?" Jordan asked. "It's not like she's someone with an archeological degree like my uncle or that creep Crowley."

Lilith cradled her hands across her stomach. "It was a matter of like attracting like, Jordan Jensen. Like Amanda Sault, Frances Tarbush was attuned to the crystal trident's unique sound vibration, like when you hear ringing in your ears, and followed the sound to the hidden compartment in the top of the arch."

Jordan's mouth twitched. "You mean the crystal trident acted like a cell phone and used a special ringtone to call her?"

"That is exactly what I mean, Jordan Jensen. Well done!" Lilith clapped.

Suddenly, Melody groaned. "Well that's bloody great. I'm related to an axe wielding criminal." Her shoulders slumped.

"Florence Whitney and Frances Tarbush are more heroes than criminals, Melody Spencer," Lilith said defensively. "They did what they needed to do in order to protect the code of time and maintain the delicate balance between the past and future. Max Tarbush threatened to expose this because of his greedy, cruel nature."

"If being a Timekeeper was such a big deal for Frances and Florence," Amanda asked, "then why was the Arch of Atlantis buried and forgotten in Melody's backyard?"

Lilith sighed deeply as she moved closer to them. "Since both women were childless, there was no one left to take over the job of Timekeeper. Thirteen years after Frances Tarbush's death, Florence Whitney, by then too old to be a Timekeeper herself, decided to bury the arch to protect it against those like Max Tarbush, who would use it for purely unscrupulous reasons." Lilith smiled. "However, I believe Florence Whitney trusted her instincts enough to know that whoever found the Arch of Atlantis would be worthy to take over the job of Timekeeper. I see she was correct."

Drake snorted. "Her instincts might have been bang on, Lilith, but those riddles she wrote are totally whacked. Why would Aunt Flo write something about a plowman's daughter needing protection from a wild arrow, under the date May fourth, 1429?"

"The Scribe must write in riddles to protect the secrets of time, Drake Bailey. When Florence Whitney traveled back through time to May fourth, 1429, she knew that the clues presented in the riddle would help her make the right decisions and take the right actions to prevent history from changing."

"So what'd the clues tell Aunt Flo to do?" Treena asked.

"Florence Whitney needed to save Joan of Arc, the plowman's daughter, from being killed in Orleans. It was not her destiny to die at the hands of an insane archer whose mind had been poisoned by Belial's influence. History has recorded her fate differently, so it was Florence Whitney's job to protect the sparrow—a term of endearment given to Joan by the peasants."

Ravi's face puckered. "How are we supposed to know all that historical junk?"

"Yeah," Drake added. "There are no satellites floating around in the past, so we can't even use our cell phones to access the net and check the facts."

Treena's jaw dropped. "Whoa! No cell phones? No texting? No tweeting? How will we cope?"

Lilith smiled. "You all must make good use of your talents. Everything you need will be revealed in a timely fashion. Know this, trust in this."

"But, Lilith, you haven't told us how we're going to fight this Belial," Melody argued. "Or even how we'll get back to the present. I know as much about being a Timekeeper as I do about brain surgery."

"Have faith, Melody Spencer. Belial is like a wild animal behind iron bars. No harm will come to you if you just observe the evil from a distance and never open the cage. The first rule as a Timekeeper is to *pay attention*, and then use the necessary *action* for the best results. You will know your Timekeeper mission is completed when the layer of time that surrounds all of you is lifted, and you find yourselves standing in front of the Arch of Atlantis. When this happens, the crystal trident must be put back into the keystone so the whirling rainbow can take you home. A word of caution—*never* take off your Babel necklaces. This is how the Arch of Atlantis locates and summons you."

"Summons us? How does it do that?" Treena asked.

"The blue stone will start to glow, then gently vibrate," Lilith explained. "So make sure it is worn next to your skin, Treena Mui."

Drake laughed. "Sounds like some kind of funky pager to me!"

Suddenly, the hairs on Amanda's neck and head tingled as if an electrical current was running through her. She shuddered. "OMG! Incoming message!" Amanda opened the Timekeepers' log and immediately jotted down whatever words popped into her mind.

"What's up with Amanda?" Jordan asked, sliding away from her.

"Time has summoned the Scribe," Lilith replied. "It means the Timekeepers are needed."

The flow of words felt so natural to Amanda, like she was born to receive them. Visions started pouring into her mind—knights on horseback, tents with colorful banners, a dark green forest, flying arrows—all bombarding her like a movie shown in fast forward. Then, as quickly as it had begun, the tingling ceased and Amanda stopped writing. She shuddered again, as the prickly sensation left her body.

"What'd you write, Amanda?" Treena asked.

Amanda glanced down into the log. She frowned.

Jordan bowed before her. "Care to share, oh mighty Scribe?"

Amanda gave Jordan a proper scowl. "Okay, but don't blame me if you're too much of a sports-goon to understand the secret code, Jockstrap." She cleared her throat to recite, *"May 1st, 1214—Games and songs and revelry, act as the cloak of devilry. So that an English legend may give to the poor, we must travel to Nottingham to even the score."*

Drake puffed his cheeks out like they were filled with a packet of pop rock candy. "Am I missing something or is that stupid riddle just as confusing to everyone else?"

Treena smirked. "So much for being a genius."

Lilith laughed softly. Then, her angelic face took on a serious expression before she said, "There is something else that must be told. The date Amanda Sault recorded is the exact day the Timekeeper mission is to occur. Not before. Not after. You will always arrive prior to the written date in order to prepare yourselves."

Jordan groaned. "Why does she have to make it sound like cramming for final exams?"

A milky white light suddenly flooded the area where everyone stood. Amanda knew it was the same radiant light that had pulled them into the Arch of Atlantis because her body felt relaxed and calm. Lilith placed her hands together, bowed before them, and took a step into the shimmering light. In that moment, Lilith's body started to vibrate so fast that her face became a blur. Then came the creepy part—Lilith gelled into the floor—sinking fast, like a slab of ice melting into boiling water.

Before Lilith completely disappeared, Amanda yelled, "But, Lilith, I still don't understand what it is that we're supposed to do!"

"You will know soon enough, Amanda Sault. Remember, all of you have special gifts you bring to each Timekeeper mission. You will know when you are required to give. All you need to do is look, listen, and trust."

As she disappeared, the marble floor they were standing on swallowed them whole.

10. *The Green Boy*

*R*ainbows. That was all Amanda saw swirling around her.

Then she caught a glimpse of the opening of the Arch of Atlantis straight ahead. It happened so fast she could barely take a breath. *Whump!* She bounced off the soft ground and rolled several feet, just missing a deformed root. Someone landed on top of her, then another, and another, until she could barely breathe. Something sharp in Jordan's backpack jabbed her in the shoulder blades. She tried to move but couldn't. Hoping her lungs wouldn't pop, Amanda smacked her open hand against the earth again and again in a silent bid to get everyone off of her.

Amanda heard Jordan laughing as he walked up behind her. She stopped her pummeling.

"What's so funny, Jockstrap?" She hissed under the pressure.

Jordan bent down and grinned. "Seeing you kiss dirt."

Amanda growled. "You'd better start running, 'cause when I get outta here, I'm gonna give you something to kiss!"

"That's quite enough!"

Amanda craned her neck. "Who said that?"

A drooping tree rustled wildly until branches were pulled away to reveal a face within the leaves. It was Melody.

"How'd you get up there, Melody?" Treena asked as she rolled off of Ravi. He groaned.

"I really have no idea," Melody replied. "All I remember is being shot out the arch and at the last moment, I flung myself upward so that I didn't smash into any of you."

"Do you need any help getting down?" Professor Lucas asked, stretching his back.

Melody shook her head, then grabbed the thickest branch within reach and swung off of it like Jane trying to outdo Tarzan. She landed with the grace of a gymnast.

"Wow, Melody, you never told us you could do that!" Drake shouted, standing up.

"Melody never told us that she had a kid, either," Amanda added, grunting to stand last.

Melody froze. Jordan gave Amanda a look that told her to go to the penalty box.

"That's not our business, Amanda," Professor Lucas said. "We all have ghosts in our closets. Let it be."

Melody nodded to the professor. "Thank you for respecting my privacy, Professor Lucas." Then she glanced back at Amanda. "You'd best do your job and retrieve the crystal trident from the keystone as Lilith instructed, Amanda."

Melody sounded curt and to the point. It was best not to offer her any comeback. Amanda turned and ran toward the Arch of Atlantis. Climbing up one side as she had done before, she reached over and grabbed the crystal trident. She had just enough time to jump down before the arch started to vibrate at such an accelerated speed that it disappeared within seconds.

Jordan rubbed his eyes. "Did you see that? The arch vanished!"

Treena moaned. "Now we're really stuck here. Doesn't Lilith know my hair can't take this kind of dampness? I'll need a hot oil treatment for sure."

"You need more than that," Ravi added. "A face lift would do for starters."

"Zip it, both of you," Professor Lucas said. "My guess is that when the crystal trident is removed during a Timekeeper mission, the arch cloaks itself until our task is completed."

Melody nodded. "Yes, your theory seems to make perfect sense, Professor Lucas."

"Look, if we're going to be fellow Timekeepers, I'd like you to call me John. Sounds less formal, don't you think?"

Melody blushed. "Yes, well then, please feel free to call me Melody, John."

Good. At least the grown-ups won't be at each other's throats. Amanda heard a bird whistle in the distance and turned toward it. Green. All she saw was the leafy green canopy of a forest. Arrows of sunlight pierced through some of the foliage, but for the most part, they were standing in a large pocket of shades and shadows. *A great setting for a slasher movie. Ravi should feel right at home here.* She took a deep breath and realized how heavy and moist the air seemed, like being in her grandmother's sweat lodge only without the perspiration dripping down her face.

"So, besides being in a forest, where are we?" Treena asked.

Jordan shrugged. "I dunno. Ask the mighty Scribe."

Amanda's guts clenched. "Look, I'm new at this Scribe thing, Jockstrap, so lay off." Then, she yanked out the Timekeepers' log from the bib of her overalls, released the clasp, flipped open the cover, and carefully inserted the crystal trident inside.

"Please, let me see the log book, Amanda," Melody requested.

As soon as it was in her hands, Melody rifled through the log until she found the correct page. She scanned the riddle, and arched a brow. "Well, we must be standing somewhere in Sherwood Forest because Nottingham is mentioned."

"Sherwood Forest?" Drake asked. "Robin Hood's Sherwood Forest?"

"It appears so, Drake," Melody said. "Amanda wrote, *So that an English legend may give to the poor*, which can only mean one historical figure—Robin Hood, who was suspected to live around the time of 1214. But I don't quite understand the first part of the message."

"May I see that, Melody?" Professor Lucas asked.

She passed him the log, and the professor perused it. "Hmm. *Games and songs and revelry*, probably means a festival and coincidently, May 1st—May Day—was one of the biggest holidays during the Middle Ages." He closed the log and returned it to Amanda.

Jordan raked his hair with his fingers. "Okay, let's replay the game plan. We're outside Nottingham, standing somewhere in Sherwood Forest, and there's gonna be a big medieval party happening soon. Belial is obviously gonna use May Day as diversion to smoke out Robin Hood. What I want to know is how are we supposed to *even the score?*"

Treena scratched her double chin. "Well, in all the movies I've watched about Robin Hood, there's usually an archery contest involved. So maybe we're here to help Robin win."

Ravi snorted. "Help *Robin Hood* win an archery contest? What's wrong with that picture, Treena? I don't know about you, but I can't remember the last time I picked up a bow and shot an arrow."

"Fine, cobra breath, I admit I'm not up to speed on archery lingo, but what about Jordan?" Treena asked. "Surely, White Pines' wonder-jock knows how to use a bow."

Jordan put up his arms. "Don't look at me. The last time I shot an arrow it went through the kitchen window and pierced the dining room table. I was grounded for a week."

"Great. So what now?" Amanda asked.

"Now we start walking toward Nottingham," Professor Lucas said, pointing to an old signpost, half-covered with vines, next to the tree Melody had jumped down from. The sign was marked *Nottingham* in bold red letters and pointed southward.

"Well, that's a start, John," Melody replied. "Lilith did say that Timekeepers observe first and then act. So let's follow the path and see if anything jumps out at us."

It was a bad choice of words. Something did jump out at them. All Amanda saw was fur and fangs charging out of the forest. A strong odor of rotting garbage followed it. Jordan dived behind the nearest bush as a huge brown dog bounded directly into his uncle and knocked him over like a bowling pin.

"Hey, mutt, get away from my uncle!" Jordan picked up a stick and waved it in the air.

The dog suddenly turned on him. It was mangy with dark brown eyes, a wet nose, and long gangly legs. Amanda covered her nose. The dog stank like spoiled fish. With a long pink tongue bobbing like a fleshy yo-yo, it started to advance on Jordan. He held out the stick as if it were a magical sword as someone crashed through the thicket. It was a boy, roughly Jordan's age, but shorter. He wore a dark green hood over his head, a long grubby shirt, and dirty brown pants that ended above the knees. Worn hose covered the rest of his legs, while a pair of leather ankle boots acted as clumsy medieval sport shoes.

The boy positioned himself between Jordan and the hairy beast. Facing the dog, he wagged a finger at it. "Bad dog, Tuck! Bad dog!"

The dog's long tail collapsed between its legs, and it shrunk to the ground in apology. The boy turned to face Jordan. "Thou canst put yon stick down. Tuck won't hurt thee, unless thou art a rabbit or a deer."

Amanda giggled. "That makes you safe, Jordan. By the way you jumped in those bushes I'd say you're more like a chicken!"

Jordan clenched his teeth. His ears went pink. He turned toward Amanda and balled his fist. "Look, Amanda, shut your face or I'll—"

Jordan stopped his tirade. The boy who rescued him from that furry monster was now aiming a loaded crossbow at his throat. Jordan's breathing was getting raspier by the second. Not taking his eyes off Jordan, the boy reached back and pulled off his green hood. A mass of reddish-brown hair tumbled out to frame his grimy face, while a pair of steady, hazel eyes never wavered from Jordan.

"Hey, kid, drop the crossbow and move away from my nephew!" Professor Lucas demanded, advancing upon both boys.

It happened in a flash. The end of a staff appeared from a bush and tripped up Professor Lucas, flattening him instantly. Another person emerged from the forest. Amanda's eyes widened. He was gigantic and had the arms of a gorilla. He must be close to seven feet tall. The giant's clothing closely matched that worn by the medieval juvenile delinquent sticking Jordan with the arrow, except that a hooded, dark-gray cape with scalloped edges covered his massive shoulders. A small white fleur-de-lis was embroidered on the left side of his cape.

"All is well, Robyn?" the giant asked calmly, as he pushed the end of his staff into the professor's chest.

"Yea, Jean," the boy replied. "I wait to hear this knave utter an apology to yon lady." He dug his arrow deeper into Jordan's skin.

Jordan winced. He dropped the stick.

Treena jumped. She stared at the huge man with her wide, almond eyes. "Did you just call him Robyn? Robyn—as in Robin Hood?"

The giant thundered out a laugh that shook the leaves. "Nay, nay. Robyn Hodekin is what he is called among friends. He shares his namesake with the devilish forest elf who seeks revenge on those who cross him. Isn't that so, Robyn?"

Robyn gave his titanic friend a scowl and then nudged Jordan again. "Apologize!"

"I suggest that you apologize to Amanda, Jordan," Melody advised. "It appears the only way out."

Jordan clenched his teeth. "Okay, okay! Sorry, Amanda!"

Amanda's lips curled with pleasure. "Apology accepted. You may release him, Sir Robyn."

Robyn blushed. He removed his crossbow from Jordan's neck. "I am not a knight, milady. But one day I shall be one."

Melody cautiously stepped forward. "And a fine knight you'll make I'm sure, Robyn. Please allow me to introduce everyone. My name is Melody Spencer. Behind me are Treena Mui, Ravi Sharma, and Drake Bailey. The girl you defended so gallantly is Amanda Sault, and the young man with such wonderful manners is Jordan Jensen."

"Such strange names and odd clothing," Robyn said. "Where art thou from?"

"White Pines," Ravi blurted.

"White Pines? I have not heard of such a place," Robyn said, scratching his chin.

"Yeah, well, it's sort of off the beaten trail," Treena replied. "Takes *time* to get there."

Robyn shot Treena a puzzled look.

"Uh, we came for the May Day celebrations," Amanda added.

"May Day? Then thou art a day early, milady Amanda," he replied.

Amanda's jaw dropped. So did most of the others. They were a day early? What were they gonna do until tomorrow? It wasn't as if they could go hang out at the local library or rent a movie from the corner store. The only thing going for them was that they'd found the famous Robin Hood before Belial. Amanda sighed. This Timekeeper thing wasn't going to be easy.

"Excuse me, but do you think you could get Goliath to back off?" Professor Lucas grunted.

Melody giggled. "Oh yes, I almost forgot, the dog lover is John Lucas."

Amanda watched Robyn's dog lick the professor across the face. He winced as gobs of doggy drool dripped from his cheek.

Robyn laughed. "Leave off, Tuck! Let the man up, Jean."

Jean spun his staff around like a seasoned pro and offered a huge hand to Professor Lucas. He took it with a little hesitation and was launched back on his feet in under a second.

The professor checked over his hand. "Thanks. Uh, Jean, is it?"

The big man smiled. "Jean le Nailor." Then he pulled back his hood to reveal short black hair, dark blue eyes, a long nose, and a strong, square jaw.

"Are you from France, Jean?" Melody inquired, pointing to the fleur-de-lis on his cloak.

Jean turned, bowed toward Melody, and said, "Yea, milady Melody. 'Tis where I met Robyn. We marched in the Crusade together."

Professor Lucas was busy brushing himself off when he abruptly stopped. "Crusade? Do you mean the Children's Crusade of 1212?" he asked in astonishment.

Robyn nodded. "My father was killed in the Crusades when I was but a child. When I became of age, my mother sent me to her relations in France to be trained as a knight. While I was there, a young man called Stephen rallied the children to take up banners and join him to recover the Holy Land. I felt it was my duty to my father to follow this brave lad."

"But didn't that Crusade end in disaster with many children losing their lives or being sold into slavery?" Professor Lucas asked.

Jean banged his staff into the ground. "Zounds, 'tis true! Many times I saw death on a child's face. Robyn and I made the journey to Marseille, only to find out that most of us were to be shipped to the east as slaves. We escaped with the help of a kind French monk called Tuck, who gave us his dog to see to our protection."

Amanda stifled a giggle. It figures. The story of Friar Tuck got all twisted around by the local rumor mongers of the middle ages. She looked down at Friar Tuck's namesake, who appeared content licking his furry privates. Amanda rolled her eyes and looked elsewhere.

"Why would you guys need Tuck for protection?" Jordan asked sarcastically. "You do just fine waving that stupid crossbow and staff around at people."

Robyn's face hardened. He tightened the grip on his crossbow. "Why dost thou ask many questions? Art thou the sheriff's spies?"

Treena laughed nervously. "Spies? Us? Good one, Robyn!"

Jean la Nailor inclined his head. "Good...one?"

"Uh, what Treena meant to say is that we've heard a lot of *good* things about *you*, Robyn," Drake explained. "Isn't that right, guys?"

Everyone nodded.

"Such as?" Robyn probed, as he deliberately pointed his crossbow at Jordan.

Jordan bit his lip. "Uh, things like...like—"

"Things like helping a damsel in distress," Amanda said, tapping her chest.

Robyn lowered his crossbow and softened his features. "I thank thee for thy kindness, milady Amanda, but truth be told, I arrived too late to help my mother."

"Why? What happened to your mother?" Drake asked softly.

Robyn sighed. "When I returned to my French relations, they had received news that my mother was ill. Jean, a shepherd by trade, had no home to go back to, so he made the journey with me to Loxley, in Warwickshire. My mother died before I got home." He paused to cross himself. "She...she was a goodly woman who cared for others. She arranged for me to stay with Sir Robert Fitzooth, a close friend of my father's, who lives in Nottingham. Sir Robert is kind, but he is ailing. To honor my mother, I help by taking care of his household needs."

Jean chuckled. "Is that so, Hodekin? Do Sir Robert's household needs include his daughter, Miriam?"

Robyn's face turned beet red.

Treena gasped. "Miriam? Maid Miriam?"

Jean grinned. "The fairest maid, according to Robyn."

Robyn threw down his crossbow and jumped the unsuspecting giant. Even Tuck backed off. Fists flew, arms flailed, and bodies rolled. Melody was there in an instant. She picked up Jean's staff, shoved it between the scrapping boys, and tried to pry them apart. It almost worked. What she hadn't counted on was Jean shifting his weight and pushing the staff back with enough force to send her sailing head first into Professor Lucas. He grimaced from the impact, as he attempted some funky dance moves backward until he stepped on top of Robyn's discarded crossbow. Click—the arrow was instantly launched.

"Duck, Ravi!" Amanda yelled.

The arrow sliced through the air. Ravi ducked as Jordan raced toward him. Amanda heard branches snapping, accompanied by a great thud that shook the ground. She looked up to catch sight of the biggest deer she'd ever seen thrashing on the ground, trying to fight off death with its long, powerful legs. The arrow had pierced its eye. It thrashed in the bushes like a salmon on a hook for all of five seconds until it lay still.

"OMG! Professor Lucas killed Bambi!" Treena screamed.

"Aye! Great shot, John!" Robyn yelled, as he roughly clapped the professor on the back. "The table will be full tonight!"

Jean guffawed. "And many nights henceforth, judging by the size of the stag, Robyn!"

A shrill whistle was heard in the distance. Amanda looked around, but there was nothing but greenery.

"Quickly, the sheriff's men approach!" Robyn said urgently. "We must hide."

"But...where?" Amanda asked, pulling Jordan's backpack closer to her shoulders.

Robyn lunged for his crossbow. "Follow me!"

Robyn and Jean headed into the forest. Tuck howled. He lobbed off in their direction, twigs and dead leaves crunched under his haste. Amanda started to feel the ground vibrate and knew it wouldn't be long before the sheriff's men arrived.

Jordan reached down, pulled Ravi up, and pushed him in front of him. "Hoof it, Sharma!"

Ravi and Melody sprinted ahead of Jordan. Amanda twisted around and waved at Drake, Treena, and Professor Lucas. "Come on, guys, before we get left behind!"

With her body in flight mode, Amanda hurdled over a stump, cleared a boulder, and dodged a fallen tree. Making headway, she ducked under a low lying branch and jumped but lost her footing and slipped. A sharp gnarled branch snagged Jordan's backpack and pulled her through the air. Her legs were moving, but she wasn't going anywhere. She felt paralyzed, a marionette to a puppet master's wicked whims, as the others bounded farther away from her. She heard a piercing scream and stopped wiggling. Terrified and trapped, Amanda became as still as the dead deer.

"Dost thou yield?" a man with a raspy voice shouted.

"We yield!" Professor Lucas answered.

The branch suspending Amanda snapped. She dropped to the forest floor like an out-of-control acorn and landed yards away from a grizzly-looking soldier in chain mail and stockings, hacking through the bushes with his sword. Scrambling behind a decaying tree trunk, Amanda hugged it, held her breath, and watched as the soldier stopped and looked her way for what seemed like an eternity before he sheathed his sword. He grunted, cleared his throat, and then horked on the ground.

"'Tis all clear!" the soldier yelled gruffly.

Shaking, Amanda let her breath go and watched him stomp back toward the others.

In the distance someone whistled out a strange code. Another whistle responded from across the tree tops. Dread punched Amanda in the stomach. She was on her own. She couldn't go forward without getting lost, she couldn't go back without getting caught. Her only option was to take Lilith's advice. *All you need to do is look, listen, and trust.* Amanda's fingers dug into the pulpy stump as she downloaded those words into her brain. She scanned the area. Only dark green shadows of the forest surrounded her, the leaves rustling back in hideous laughter.

11. The Hunchback of Nottingham

"Poachers!" a soldier yelled.

From her post under the thick, sheltering bushes, Amanda followed the soldier's pointing finger with the pair of small binoculars she'd scrounged from Jordan's backpack. She focused in. The soldier was pointing toward the deer Robyn's arrow had slain.

"Aye. The sheriff will be pleased with our arrest," another soldier said.

Drake shook his head. "But…it was an accident, we—"

"Silence!" a third soldier growled.

Amanda did a headcount. There were six soldiers total. One of the soldiers jumped off his horse and walked toward the deer with a thick, bristly rope in his hand. A few minutes later he was back on his gray steed and kicking at its muscular flanks like a man possessed. Snapping and cracking bushes accompanied the deer as it was mercilessly dragged out of the forest and down the path.

Their gruff laughter made Amanda cringe. "Up with thee! Start walking!"

Treena was on the ground in tears, her high-heeled black sandal caught under a gigantic root system. Amanda shook her head. *When will Treena learn not to be so fashion conscious?* Drake was wringing his hands and kept looking back toward where the others had run off. Professor Lucas helped Treena up and guided her to solid ground.

He gently patted her shoulder. "It'll be okay, Treena. It's not your fault."

Drake snorted. "No, not at all. It was the tree root's fault for not moving out of the way fast enough."

"That's enough, Drake," Professor Lucas said. "What's done is done."

"Aye," the soldier snapped, "and thou wilt wish thy life was over when the sheriff is done with thee."

The soldiers laughed. Amanda gagged. It sounded like chunks of gristle were caught in their throats.

The soldiers arranged themselves so that two rode in front of Treena, Drake, and Professor Lucas, then one on each side of them, and one behind. The sixth soldier dragging the deer had long gone. Amanda bit her bottom lip. She felt as circled and trapped as they were. Before setting out after them, she searched the area behind her with the binoculars. *Why haven't the others come back?*

After what seemed like hours, Amanda welcomed the warmth of the sun on her face and arms, as she left the dark, leafy forest behind and walked into a rolling, grassy meadow. Her nostrils flared in appreciation. Even the air seemed less heavy than it had been in the forest. Treena, Drake, Professor Lucas, and the soldiers were about to enter the town of Nottingham. Amanda continued to keep out of sight. She pulled out the binoculars again and checked over the area. Stalls and carts were being set up all around the grounds. Laughter and singing accompanied the vendors. A tall knotted pole, stripped of its bark and branches, was set into the ground in the middle of the activity. At the top of the pole, streams of thick ribbons spiraled around the pole like a rainbow-colored serpent. Most of the buildings looked like huge wooden tents with whitewashed woven twigs for walls and very steep roofs. Plumes of black smoke billowed out of many of the crooked stone chimneys. Amanda caught a faint whiff of burned meat and singed fur.

"This way!" the lead soldier shouted.

The soldiers led their captives over a stone bridge, down a ravine, then up a small hill and to a drawbridge. Amanda's breath lodged in her throat when she saw that the professor and her classmates were standing in front of a massive stone castle situated on a high rock. The sandy-toned rock was pummeled with grooves and gouges. Tall towers commandeered the corners like possessed chess pieces. The castle gateway was flanked by two drum towers. Slit windows stared back at her like hungry vampire bats in a cave. She gulped as one of the soldiers signaled for entrance.

Her shoulders tensed. *Great. How am I gonna get in that castle?* The soldiers herded Treena, Drake, and Professor Lucas past the gate. An ox-driven wagon overflowing with straw entered next, followed by a group of finely-dressed villagers carrying instruments that resembled guitars, then finally a cart filled with sacks and bread pulled by two gray draft horses was allowed passage before the castle gate closed. Amanda lowered the binoculars and let her head rest against the lenses. Her stomach clenched. *If I could only pass for a local, then maybe I'd be able to get through the gate.* Then she lifted her head, as her eyes widened. Lilith's words strummed through her mind, like a finely-tuned instrument. *The first rule as a Timekeeper is to pay attention, and then use the necessary action for the best results.*

She quickly peeled off Jordan's backpack, stashed the binoculars in a side pocket, then pulled out Jordan's heavy, hooded purple sweatshirt. Robyn had a shirt with a hood, and so did Jean. Many of the other villagers she'd spotted walking around the grounds also had hooded attire, so Amanda figured Jordan's hooded sweatshirt would make the perfect disguise for blending in. She lifted it over her head and struggled into it. She felt like she was being swallowed alive by a whale. The sweatshirt hung off of her like a dilapidated sail with no wind.

"Really?" she growled, flailing the long, bulky sleeves around.

Then Amanda stopped. If she'd learned anything from Treena in the last two weeks, it was how to accessorize and accentuate. *Make your clothing work for you, not against you, girl,* the drama queen had preached. She pulled off the sweatshirt and reached for the backpack. Making sure all the zippers were zipped and secure, Amanda shrugged it on, tightened the straps, then picked up the sweatshirt and attempted to wear it again. This time it fit much better, as the backpack took up most of the slack. Pleased with herself, she pulled the hood over her head, took a deep breath, and started walking toward the castle gate.

She heard the odd gasp among the swirl of barnyard noises and hackneyed singing. A few people crossed themselves over and over again, as if they had some kind of a flea infestation. A couple of clucking chickens crossed her path at the same time she felt someone tap her across the top of her back. She whirled around to catch a boy, perhaps a little older than her, running away. She frowned, turned back, and continued on the uneven path, sidestepping potholes, street sewage, and wagon wheel ruts.

"Poor rogue," a toothless woman said, trundling up to Amanda. She reached out with a gnarled hand, touched her back, and muttered what Amanda thought was some kind of prayer.

Then she placed a piece of bread in Amanda's hand, and ambled off in the opposite direction. Puzzled, Amanda reached over her shoulder to check if something was stuck on her back. Nope. Only a hump where the backpack was positioned was there. She shook her head, shoving the bread into the front pouch of the sweatshirt. This was getting weird.

A sudden, foul odor of dung and sweat arrested her senses. She covered her nose.

"I beg of thee," a weak voice called out.

Amanda looked around. "Who said that?"

"'Tis me, in this pit."

To the left side of the bumpy road, Amanda saw a large dug out hole. Rotten vegetables dotted the edge. She cautiously walked over and peered into the pit. A grizzled old man stared up at her. His eyes were clouded and his white hair matted with mud. His clothes were so dirty and tattered she couldn't tell what color they once were. Amanda's eyes widened.

"What are you doing down there?" she asked.

"Couldn't pay me taxes," he wheezed.

Amanda's eyebrows crinkled. "You didn't pay your taxes, so you were thrown down there? What kind of justice is that?"

The old man shrugged. "Sheriff's justice."

Amanda felt a hand touch her back, and then another, almost pushing her into the pit. She stumbled and turned as two boys fled away. She frowned. "What's with everyone touching my back?"

"Thou art a hunchback," the old man answered, coughing.

"So?"

The man looked up at her strangely. "Thou bringest luck to those not stricken."

"Stricken with what?"

He scratched his nose with a crooked finger. "Stricken with evil, child. Thou dost not know to touch thy hump wards off the evil thou art cursed with?"

Amanda sighed. She wasn't about to get into an argument with a man who was worse off than she was. She shook her head and looked at the castle. "I could use some luck of my own about now."

"Such as?" the man asked. He sounded genuine, as if he cared about her plight.

"I need to get into the castle. My friends are in there. I have to find a way to rescue them."

The wizened man was silent for the moment, while all the other archaic sounds around Amanda clashed into a mixture of medieval stew: drunks guffawing, women screeching, children crying, dogs howling, and people bartering bubbled all around her.

"I know a way," he said with a gravelly voice. "I was once a castle guard. Yonder are passages under the rock. They will lead thee into the castle courtyard."

"How do I get there?"

The man held out a hand to her. His eyes were pleading. She heard his stomach release a visceral growl. Fumbling for the piece of the bread she'd stuffed into the pouch, Amanda tossed it to him. He devoured it like a wolf would a newborn carcass.

He wiped his whiskered chin with a grimy hand. "Thou must wend thy way around the castle walls, past the last tower by the river and count one hundred paces until thou seest a big rotting stump. 'Twill be thick with moss and covered in vines and bramble. Thither, just beyond this stump, is me hole."

"Your hole?" Amanda asked.

The corners of his eyes crinkled and he flashed Amanda a black-toothed grin. "Aye. 'Tis how I stole me wenches in."

She rolled her eyes. "That's way too much information, mister."

He coughed. "Me name's Mortimer."

She smiled and waved. "Hi, Mortimer, I'm Amanda. And thanks...for the luck."

As she turned to leave, she heard Mortimer harshly hack. "If thou meetest with any resistance, Amanda," he said, his voice now strong and clear, "tell the rogues Mortimer sent thee."

As Amanda got closer to her only way into the castle, the crowds started to thin, the noises waned, the sun moved to the suppertime position, and her surroundings got greener. She took a deep welcoming breath and started to count off one hundred paces as Mortimer had instructed.

"...ninety-eight, ninety-nine, one hundred." Amanda stopped and pulled back her hood. She searched the area, and frowned. No moss-covered stump. No vines. No bramble.

She heard a sharp snap behind her. Slowly, she glanced over her shoulder. A girl with long brown braided hair stood behind her, holding a drawn longbow. An arrow was poised at the ready and aimed at Amanda. The girl was about a year older than her and seemed to possess a rough edge, yet looked feminine at the same time. A green garment which looked like an extra-long T-shirt with bat-wing sleeves covered her slim body, while a thick leather belt stuffed with three arrows held her shirt neatly in place. Like the people of this time period, she too sported a hooded woolen cloak around her shoulders. Besides the belt and arrows, her only other accessory was a coarse brown satchel that hung over one shoulder. Amanda spied the heel of a long loaf of bread and a few carrot tops protruding from the satchel.

"Be on thy way, hunchback," she said in an unwavering voice.

Amanda turned around and put up her hands. "Wait! Doncha wanna touch my hump...for luck?"

The brown-haired girl slightly lowered her bow "Nay. The last time I touched a rogue like thee I fell and twisted my foot. Leeches were applied, and I limped for a month."

Amanda scrunched her face. "Eww. Why leeches?"

The girl raised her brows. "God's wounds, simpkin, leeches take thy bad blood and leave the good. Now take thy leave or thou willst need more than just leeches to stop the bleeding!"

"But...I gotta get into the castle!" Amanda pleaded. "It's a matter of life and death!"

"'Tis none of my concern, hunchback." She pulled her bow string back farther.

Amanda felt beads of sweat trickling down her back. "Mortimer sent me!"

Startled, the girl lowered her bow. Her earth-brown eyes looked Amanda over. "If good Mortimer trusts a rogue such as thee, then I shall do the same. Follow me and stay close."

"Huh? Follow you where?"

"'Tis this way, hunchback," she said curtly, disarming the bow and placing it snugly around her shoulders. Then the girl darted off the beaten path and past a pile of neatly stacked boulders.

"By the way, I have a name. It's Amanda," she huffed, running after her.

"Miriam. Miriam Fitzooth," she replied without stopping.

Amanda almost tripped up. "Miriam? Robyn Hodekin's Miriam?"

Miriam stopped. She turned around slowly. "Thou knowest Robyn, Amanda?"

Amanda nodded. "We met today, in Sherwood Forest. He...he sort of defended my honor. He's very sweet in a pushy medieval way."

Miriam smiled. "Aye. Robyn is kind to those stricken and poor. He makes sure the lepers have bread and water every other morrow, and fashions canes for the lame and elderly of the village. He is truly his mother's son, bless her soul." She crossed herself three times.

"Yeah, well, Robyn will be the one who's stricken if I don't get into the castle and find where those soldiers took my fellow Timeke—er, friends."

Miriam's face hardened. "Robyn stricken? Dost thou jest?"

Amanda sighed. "I wish. Let's just say he'll have more to worry about than getting arrested for poaching. Trust me, Miriam, I'm here to help him."

Miriam hesitated for an instant, then as if a wall of ice melted between them, she grabbed Amanda by the elbow and led her to a gigantic stump pushed up against a steep pitted wall. The stump was plastered with moss, with vines and brambles choking it beyond death. On one side, there was a split in the trunk big enough for her to wiggle inside. Miriam pushed Amanda through it and followed her in. The stringy arms of moss dangling from all sides made Amanda feel like she was in a hollowed-out jack-o-lantern. A huge gaping hole above, plus an assortment of small irregular holes where birds had pummeled the stump, allowed enough light in for Amanda to see. Cringing, she moved away from the rotting walls, while Miriam rolled aside a huge piece of bark and let it drop to the spongy floor.

"Come hither," she said urgently.

"Come where?"

Miriam turned, bent her head, and disappeared into a carved-out hole in the wall. Amanda gulped. She had seen plenty of horror movies that started out this way. She shivered as she entered the cave, feeling the dampness penetrating through to her bones. Darkness instantly snuffed her vision. All Amanda could do was listen, feel, and trust. The sound of Miriam's breathing ahead put her at ease. Putting out her hands to stop herself from stumbling, Amanda pushed against the cave wall. It felt soft and powdery like sand. She pushed harder, felt her hands moisten and started to feel chilled. It wasn't a freezing temperature, but more like a cool spring morning.

"Does Robyn know you do this kind of stuff, Miriam?"

She stopped. Amanda almost fell over her. "What *stuff?*"

Amanda regained her balance. "You know...sneaking into the castle stuff."

Miriam giggled. "Nay, 'tis my own penance. I steal in food for the prisoners and give them comfort. Now come, we're almost thither."

Amanda let out a thankful breath as they rounded a smooth corner. A flicker of light danced across a wall ahead of them. It was another opening that led into another tunnel. She started to hear voices. Familiar voices. The closer they got to the opening, the louder the voices became. Miriam collapsed to her stomach, and just before she wiggled around another corner, she beckoned Amanda to approach. There was barely enough room for the two girls to fit side by side, with Miriam's bow digging into Amanda's ribs and Jordan's backpack sliding to one side. The hole must have shrunk at least a foot in diameter. Miriam put a finger to her lips and pulled back a piece of tattered burlap covering the hole.

"Look, Treena, it's your fault we're stuck in this stinking rat hole!"

Amanda's eyes widened when she saw the back of two jean-clad legs dangling in front of her. A wicked smell—probably from the dirty straw strewn across the floor—made her balk. Amanda nudged

Miriam and pointed. *My friends,* she mouthed to her. Miriam nodded.

"My fault? Correct me if I'm wrong, brain-drain, but I believe I was the one who had to hurdle over you to avoid doing a slam dance with each other!"

Drake snorted. "Yeah, but if you weren't following me so closely—"

"That's enough!" Professor Lucas said.

Miriam started to worm her way back to the main tunnel. She motioned Amanda to stay, and then disappeared into the darkness. Suddenly, Amanda heard a low, raspy laugh.

"Tsk, tsk...now I know why some mothers eat their young."

The professor gasped. "Crowley! You son-of—"

"Uh-ah, not in front of the children, John," the man whom Professor Lucas had called Crowley, interrupted. "Oh, and it is *Sheriff* Crowley now. Didn't you hear? I'm the *new* Sheriff of Nottingham."

"You're...the what?" the professor asked, his voice catching in his throat.

Curious, Amanda crawled closer to the opening. A long wooden bench was positioned above the hole. Drake's legs obscured her vision, so she craned her head as far as she could to get a glimpse of Professor Lucas's archenemy. Lit torches hanging from the cave walls offered minimal lighting, but enough for Amanda to catch the corners of Crowley's thin lips creeping up his face. This douche had bad news written all over him. He wasn't dressed like he came from their century at all. A long, purple cloak with matching hose and pointy shoes covered Crowley's wiry body, while his jet hair was pulled back into a small pony tail to reveal stone-gray eyes and a neatly trimmed beard. Then a glimmer just below his neckline caught Amanda's attention and held it. It was a Babel necklace, a replica of what she and the others were wearing, only Crowley's blue stone appeared darker, as if a shadow lurked inside.

"You heard me well enough, Lucas," Crowley replied. His eyes darted first to Drake, and then to Treena. "I see you've been reduced to babysitting, Johnny-boy. But, I guess there aren't many job opportunities for a disgraced professor, are there?"

"I really don't know, Marcus, you tell me. You're the *professor* who disappeared with the Mayan Arch."

"Ah, yes, but you're the *professor* they blamed," Crowley sneered.

Amanda heard Treena whimper. "I don't suppose we get our one phone call?"

"Phone call, alas no, but your well-being? Now that depends on Professor Lucas," he said.

"What the devil are you talking about, Crowley?" Professor Lucas asked.

Crowley bent his head like a cobra about to strike. "I want the crystal trident that you used to get here."

Amanda's shoulders tensed. She clutched her chest and felt the impression of the Timekeepers' log under the thickness of Jordan's sweatshirt. Good. The log and crystal trident were both safely tucked in her bib. She released a low sigh and her shoulders at the same time.

"Crystal trident? What crystal trident? You kids know what he's talking about?"

"Un-uh. Don't know nothing 'bout no crystal trident," Treena replied, shrugging.

"Me neither, chump," Drake added.

"Do you think I'm stupid?" Crowley thundered.

"I do," Drake replied. Amanda imagined him with a full-on smirk.

Professor Lucas stood up. "Look, Crowley, we have no idea what you're talking about so just let the kids go—"

"You lie like a rug, Lucas!" Crowley hissed. "I know you've been to Atlantis. I also know that there are more Timekeepers hiding out in Sherwood Forest. Face it, John, it's only a matter of time until all seven of you will occupy this dungeon."

"But we need the crystal trident to get back home," Treena pleaded.

"That's not my concern, girl," Crowley replied maliciously. "All I know is from the moment you became Timekeepers, you went against Belial."

"What happened to you, Marcus? You had a promising career, and you blew it! What has Belial promised you that you couldn't have worked for and gotten by yourself?"

Crowley stroked his greasy beard and smiled. "Knowledge, John. A firsthand knowledge of history. I could never have achieved that by keeping my nose buried in text books or going on pointless archaeological digs with feeble-minded colleagues. What humankind has destroyed in the past, I can witness with my own eyes and change it. I can *become* history! I can rewrite it!"

"But you can't *change* history! It's already been written!" Professor Lucas argued.

Crowley laughed defiantly. "That's where you're wrong, Johnny-boy. I've already changed history. I *am* the Sheriff of Nottingham. Belial has transported me here to eliminate the famous Robin Hood by any means I see fit."

Amanda's eyes bugged. It was a good thing Miriam didn't hear that. She would have gone all medieval on Crowley with her bow and arrow and attitude.

Professor Lucas took a step forward. "Why? What would be the point?"

Two guards shuffled closer to Crowley.

"Think, John, think," Crowley said, tapping a thin finger on Professor Lucas's forehead. "If the legendary Robin Hood never existed, then the ripple effect caused by his actions would be suppressed forever."

"What's that twisted lame-o talking about, Prof?" Drake asked.

Professor Lucas's shoulders sagged. "If there was no such person to rob from the rich and give to the poor, then there would be no champion—no symbol of hope—for the common people in this time period. That's what the legend of Robin Hood is really all about—fighting back and standing up against the evils of an archaic system."

"Very good, Lucas. I see the teacher has become the pupil," Crowley said, clapping.

"So what happened to the *true* Sheriff of Nottingham?" Treena asked.

"Belial has other *plans* for him, just as he does for John Lucas."

"What kind of plans?" Drake asked suspiciously.

"I wouldn't worry, brat," Crowley said, sneering. "Belial's plans don't include children. To him, the young ones are just a waste of time."

"You low-life snake!" Professor Lucas seethed. He lunged for Crowley's throat.

A guard was there in an instant and slammed the hilt of his sword into the back of the professor's skull. Treena screamed as Professor Lucas slumped to his knees and collapsed on the dirty straw floor.

Amanda jerked as she visually searched for any signs of consciousness, but he was out cold.

Crowley motioned for the guard. "Take him to the deepest cavern," he commanded.

He skulked over to Drake and Treena. Amanda swallowed hard, feeling utterly helpless. Her nails dug into the sandstone. Her throat and stomach tightened as she anticipated Crowley's next move.

"Take off those pretty necklaces and give them to me," Crowley demanded.

"But we need them to talk to people, and to get back home!" Treena cried.

Crowley drew a bejeweled dagger from his belt and lunged for Drake. He pulled him up and placed the dagger under Drake's throat. Amanda covered her mouth to keep from crying out.

Drake grunted. "Give him the stupid necklace, Treena!"

Treena whimpered as she handed her Babel necklace to him. Crowley helped himself to Drake's necklace and then roughly pushed him down to the bench. He stuffed the pair of necklaces into a pouch hanging from a leather belt around his waist. With a warning look to both Drake and Treena, he backed away, snickering.

"I-I'm scared, Drake. What's gonna happen?" Treena whispered.

Amanda could actually hear Drake swallow, feel his animosity leach down to her. "Chaos, Treena. Chaos is gonna happen."

Crowley blinked. "What did you say?"

"You heard me, nut-bar," Drake replied, through clenched teeth. "Timekeepers are here to create chaos so order can continue. Face it, Crowley, you might as well give up now."

"My, such big words for such a young mouth."

"Drake's a genius," Treena said. "That means he's smarter than you, douche-bag."

Crowley's mouth twitched like a voodoo doll's pin was stuck in his face.

Another guard stumbled up. In his hand was an iron rod with the letter B positioned at the tip. "I've brought the branding iron thou hast demanded, Sheriff."

"W-What's that for?" Treena squeaked.

Crowley's face lit up with an ugliness Amanda had never seen before. "Here, in Nottingham, we use a branding iron to keep criminals in line. The letter reveals the crime to the public. And, since you went against Belial, I thought a nice charred B on each cheek would remind you of who you are dealing with." He snapped his fingers. "Guard, chain these two criminals to the wall and encourage them to tell me what I want to know." With that, he whirled around and headed down a low-lit tunnel.

Amanda watched in silent horror as the shadows swallowed Crowley completely.

12. The Wandering Jongleur

"**N**o, no, wait, you can't do this!" Treena screamed. "I plead the fifth! I want a lawyer!"

The guard snorted like a hog and pulled Treena off the bench. Her high-heeled sandals dug into the floor, but it was no use. She stumbled and was dragged to the opposite side of the cave. Amanda struggled to peer around Drake's legs. A row of iron chains hung against the far wall. Shredded clothing and clumps of hair on the floor made Amanda feel like she was holed up in a serial killer's basement. Her throat tightened as she attempted to control her breathing.

"Let me go, you—you bully in chain mail!" Drake yelled as he was yanked off the bench.

The guard who'd brought the branding iron dropped it into a bucket of hot coals. Amanda heard a sizzle, pop, and a hiss as the coals merged with the metal. She found the courage to open her mouth, take a deep breath, and—inhaling the stench of rancid straw and rat poop—she sneezed, and sneezed again.

The struggling stopped. Amanda heard clomping head toward her and the bench was wrenched away from the wall. She stared at a pair of leather boots and dingy stockings. She tried to wiggle her way back in the hole, but the guard grabbed both her hands and plucked her out as if she was a rabbit in a magician's hat.

"Look what we have," the guard sneered, his grip acting like a pair of medieval handcuffs.

"Aye, 'tis a hunchback whose luck hath run dry," the guard added as he chained Drake.

"Amanda!" Treena yelled.

Drake laughed. "Now you two lame-brains will be sorry you messed with Timekeepers! Call in the cavalry, Amanda!"

The guard holding Amanda guffawed. Half his teeth were missing, the other half were blackened. A conical helmet covered his bulging head, while metallic fish netting draped his gray tunic. He applied pressure to her wrists. She winced.

"A-A-About that, Drake, you see—"

"Unhand the hunchback, rogue!"

Amanda looked around the guard's stout body. There, in the entranceway to another room, stood Miriam, pointing an arrow at the guard. Her hood was up to cover her face.

"Put down yon bow, and 'twill be easy on thee, rogue!" the guard growled.

"I think not, knotty-pated simpkin!" Miriam let her arrow fly.

The guard wailed as Miriam's arrow pierced his behind. "Arrgh, me arse!"

He released his hold on Amanda, and she swiftly jumped up and pulled the top of his helmet down to cover his eyes. Then she spun him around like a top and pushed him into the wall, head first. He smashed into it, wobbled, and fell back into a pile of foul smelling straw. A black rat the size of a house cat squealed and scampered out of the heap. Miriam took another arrow from her belt, placed it in her bow, and aimed it at the second guard.

He chortled wickedly, grabbed Treena by the hair, and pulled her over as far as the chains would allow. He stepped behind her and drew out his sword. "Drop thy bow, or I slit this wench's throat!"

Treena whimpered. "Now would be a good time for a knight in shining armor!"

Miriam slowly lowered her bow. She cast her eyes over to Amanda and smiled at her. Amanda frowned. She looked over toward Treena, who was being used as a human shield. A short shadow danced across the opposite wall. Her eyes widened.

Somehow Drake had escaped out of his chains. Amanda glanced back at Miriam and discreetly nodded.

"This is so you don't forget who you're messing with, chump!" Drake shouted, shoving the red-hot branding iron into the guard's cheek. "FYI—the B is for bozo!"

"Ahhhh!" the guard screeched, dropping his sword and coddling his cheek.

Drake kicked the sword away, lunged for the key ring hanging off his belt, and unlocked Treena's chains. "Will a black knight in a red dragon T-shirt do instead?" he asked, grinning.

Treena threw her arms around Drake's neck. "You bet, Sir Drake! Thanks! BTW—how'd you get out of those chains?"

Drake squirmed out of Treena's grip. "They just slid off my wrists. I guess they don't get too many criminals in my size."

Amanda raced to the fallen guard. She grabbed one hand, while Treena took the other, and together they chained him to the wall.

"So what's with the Quasimodo look?" Treena whispered, nudging her chin toward the hump.

"I had to blend in," Amanda explained quietly. "Instead, I ended up standing out. If it wasn't for meeting Miriam, I'd still be wandering around the forest. She helped me get into the castle, and saved both your butts."

Treena gasped. "Not *the* Miriam?"

"Yes, that one," Amanda whispered.

"Good," Drake murmured. "Maybe she can help us find the others."

"That's the plan," Amanda muttered.

"Please, I beg thee, unchain me too."

Miriam raised her bow. "Who speaks?"

"'Tis me, Alan a'Dale, o'er hither."

Amanda turned and noticed a carved out niche in the darkest part of the dungeon. She grabbed a torch off the wall and walked over with Miriam. A young man, maybe sixteen, was chained to the wall, his arms and legs pulled as far apart as they would go. He wore a funny looking red cap, the kind a jester might wear, which covered most of his curly black hair, a dingy white shirt decorated with large shiny buttons on both sleeves, and tight green breeches which were unevenly stuffed into a pair of long boots. A pear-shaped guitar-like instrument lay in the corner, propped up against Treena's knapsack.

"Take me with thee," Alan a'Dale begged.

Amanda looked at Miriam, who lowered her bow.

"What hast thou done to anger the sheriff?" She asked.

He sighed. "'Tis the truth, I am but a lowly jongleur. I was arrested for singing a ballad."

"A ballad? About what?" Amanda asked, furrowing her brow.

He grinned. Even in the low light of the flickering torch, his teeth were white and straight. "In Nottingham, the people fight," he sang eloquently. "They cry for justice from their king. But no one hears the beggar's plight. Only feel the sheriff's cruel, sharp sting."

Miriam laughed. "'Tis my kind of song! Release the jongleur, Amanda."

Amanda snatched the key ring out of Drake's hand and passed the torch to him. As she started to unlock Alan a'Dale's shackles, she met his sky blue eyes dead on.

"Thou art the prettiest hunchback my eyes hath seen," he whispered to her.

Amanda could feel her body ping all over. Pockets of warmth erupted through her skin in places she never knew existed.

"We must make haste, Amanda," Miriam said, severing her private thoughts. "Before more guards appear."

Amanda nodded. "Can you take us to Robyn?"

Even under the hood, Amanda caught Miriam frowning. "Thou saidest Robyn would be stricken if thou didn't get into the castle to find thy friends. Now, thou hast found them. Why dost thou need me to take thee to Robyn?" Her fingers tightened around her bow.

"What's going on, Amanda?" Treena asked. "She sounds freaked."

Amanda pursed her lips. "Miriam wants answers. I sort of told her that Robyn would be stricken if I didn't find you guys."

Drake groaned. "Something tells me that we're the ones who are gonna be stricken."

"Why dost thy friends speak so oddly, Amanda?" Miriam asked suspiciously.

"Aye, sounds like the devil 'imself sits upon their tongues," Alan a'Dale added, as he picked up his instrument and plucked it.

Miriam aimed her arrow at Amanda. "God's wounds, hath a hunchback tricked me again? I will do no leeches for thee!"

Startled, Amanda dropped the key and put her hands up. No use explaining that the only way she could understand Miriam was because of her Babel necklace. She glanced nervously at Drake and Treena, then something Alan a'Dale had just said hit her.

"No wait, Miriam, Alan is right. The truth is that both my friends have been bewitched by Sheriff Crowley. He used dark magic to strike their voices, and now he seeks to take away your people's hope. Crowley is evil and doesn't belong in Nottingham. We're really secret *law keepers* sent here to stop him. Trust me, Miriam, Robyn and the rest of the people of Nottingham, will only be safe when we accomplish what we came here to do."

Drake smiled. "I hate to admit this, Amanda, but that was pure genius."

Miriam sighed. She relaxed her stance, loosened her arrow, and lowered her bow. "Very well, Amanda. Thy plea rings true. Sheriff Crowley hath been in Nottingham for over a fortnight, and hence, I hath not seen Sheriff Philip Marc. 'Tis the truth, Sheriff Crowley hath caused nothing but grief and anger. I shall do as thou biddest. But I warn thee, if thither be a drop of deceit, 'twill be unlucky for thee and thy friends."

Chains rattled behind them. "Thou rogues shall pay dearly for this," the shackled guard hissed, coming out of his stupor. "Guards! Hither! Help!"

Drake dropped the torch, scooped up some rags off the floor, and shoved them in the guard's mouth. Then he picked up the key ring, grinned, and tossed it into the bucket of hot coals. "Told ya we're here to create chaos, lame-brain!"

"I know of a tunnel leading to the courtyard," Alan a'Dale whispered.

"Art thou mad?" Miriam snapped. "We will be marked."

"Nay. We shall be merry with the crowd," Alan a'Dale said, strutting toward the entrance to the main tunnel, his instrument slapping against his back. "Come hither, quickly."

Amanda could hear faint footsteps coming down the opposite end of the tunnel.

Treena lunged for her backpack and strapped it on.

"Where are we going, Amanda?" Drake asked.

Amanda wanted to say "crazy," but instead said, "Apparently, to be merry."

"Mary? Who's Mary?" Treena asked, as she stumbled up the tunnel.

An expansive courtyard filled with people, wagons, tents, and livestock greeted Amanda at the mouth of the tunnel. Dusk was pressing in on them as the sun's shimmering farewell poked through the thick rising smoke of nearby fires. The courtyard was a beehive of activity, so it was easy to blend in. Musicians were playing odd-looking string instruments, some similar to what Alan a'Dale owned, while other instruments resembled flutes or reeds or bells. As they merged with the crowd, the sound of laughter and noisy bartering rose above the music. Wagons loaded with fine fabrics, fruits, vegetables, cheeses, and breads were scattered about chaotically.

"We shall make for the minstrels' tent," Alan a'Dale said. "The harp player is my coz."

Miriam tugged on his instrument. "Thou hath better not lead us on a merry chase, jongleur," she warned.

"If milady dost not let go of my lute, then 'twill be me chasing thee," he growled.

Miriam nodded sharply, released the instrument he'd called a lute, then gave Amanda, Drake, and Treena the come along sign with her chin. They had gotten halfway through the courtyard when a brawl broke out near a fish stand, knocking a barrel of fish all over the ground. The screech of fighting roosters in a small pen next to Amanda made her jump. People were yelling at the birds, rousing them, and gambling on which one would win. Disgusted, she whirled around, and couldn't find Miriam or Alan a'Dale anywhere.

"Where'd they go?" Amanda asked.

"I dunno," Treena said, glancing all around. "There are hundreds of people all around us, and it's getting dark."

"Yeah," Drake added. "Plus there's about a hundred foot by fifteen foot thick stone wall surrounding us. I don't see us getting outta here any time soon."

Before Amanda could say anything, someone slapped her square on the back. She stumbled and clenched her teeth. She was tired of being the town's punching bag. Seeing a slim, long-bodied, mottled brown fish by her foot, she stooped to pick it, then turned and walloped whoever smacked her.

"Umph! Why dost thou hit me with a ling, hunchback?" a portly boy asked, rubbing his ruddy cheek. He sounded more puzzled than angry.

He reached over, grabbed Amanda by both shoulders, and lifted her off the ground. She dropped the fish and stared at the droopy-eyed boy, who somehow resembled a loyal hunting dog with brown matted hair. He wasn't threatening, but he wasn't exactly friendly either. Sugar caked the corners of his mouth, and he wore a rumpled green tunic like a potato sack. His breath smelled surprisingly sweet.

Drake kicked at the hulking boy. "Let her go, Oxzilla!"

Treena picked up another fish and swung it around in the air. "Prepare to become sushi-ized, douche-bag!"

The boy turned his big head slightly. "Thou mumblest oddly. Did thy tongues get cut out and shoved in backwards?"

Amanda groaned. "He doesn't understand you guys!"

"Well understand this, lunk-head!" Treena yelled as she whacked him across the back of the head with the fish.

The next thing Amanda felt was her butt kissing the ground. She winced. Enough was enough. She was getting tired of playing the stricken fool game. Amanda rolled to her feet and, struggling out of Jordan's hooded sweater, grunted and groaned until it lay in a heap at her feet. Then she pulled off his knapsack.

"There! Satisfied? I'm no more a hunchback than you're Robyn Hodekin!"

The boy scrunched his face. "Wot, me? Robyn Hodekin? Nay, nay, I'm Much the Miller's son. Robyn's yonder."

Amanda blinked her eyes. "Robyn is here? In the castle grounds?"

The boy nodded slowly. "Aye. Stole 'im in in me bread cart wit' the others."

"The...others?" Amanda gasped.

In that same moment, the fish Treena was swinging slipped out of her hands and into the face of a nearby castle guard as he started up the closest hill.

Drake groaned. "Great, Treena, out of all the guards, you had to hit one who captured us in the forest."

The guard wiped his face and growled. Then his eyes bugged. "Poachers!" he yelled, pointing at Treena and Drake.

Great. Amanda groaned. *Where's a pair of ruby shoes when you need them?*

"Wait a sec," Treena said, poking Amanda and Drake. "What happens in every action movie that gets the hero out of a jam?"

"Knowing a form of martial arts?" Drake asked.

"Knowing how to use a paperclip as a lethal weapon?" Amanda added.

Treena rolled her eyes. "No, there's always a diversion created so the hero can escape and go save the world."

"Treena, you're brilliant," Amanda said, snapping her fingers. Swiftly she put the knapsack back on, bent down, picked up Jensen's sloughed sweatshirt, and headed for the fighting roosters.

She kicked over the pen, then using the sweatshirt as if it was a matador's cape, Amanda herded the birds straight into the path of the oncoming guard. One of the roosters flew up and started pecking at the guard's bulbous nose. The other rooster went for his fat fingers. He screamed medieval obscenities while the people clapped and laughed. They started betting against the guard and cheering for the birds. Amanda dropped the hoody, grabbed the guard's purse off his belt, opened it, and threw whatever money was in it into the air. The crowd hollered and stampeded wherever the money landed. A few coins rolled under a bread cart and people pushed and pulled until the cart was knocked over onto its side. The two draft horses attached to the cart reared and raced away, spilling sacks of flour and baked breads behind them.

"Me cart!" The miller's son roared, chasing after his horses.

"Get off my head, Sharma!" Amanda heard the voice coming from underneath a burlap sheet where the cart had toppled.

"Then get your knee outta my privates, Jenson!" Another voice replied.

Amanda's jaw dropped. "Jockstrap? Ravi?"

"Amanda?" the two voices yelled in unison.

Relief flooded her insides. "Yeah, it's me! Drake and Treena are here too!"

"A-Amanda?" Alan a'Dale uttered from behind her. He spun Amanda around to face him. His eyes widened. "Thou…thou art no hunchback." Then he produced a full-on grin and said, "Thou art comely. Thou shalt be my muse!"

"I'm not sure what he's saying, but by the way he's checking you out, it looks like you're gonna need a restraining order soon," Treena said, plucking up Jordan's sweatshirt.

"Did I just hear Jordan?" Drake asked excitedly as he joined them.

Amanda nodded. "Jordan and Ravi were smuggled in in Much's bread cart."

Suddenly people started screaming and backing away. A small girl, dirty-faced and wide-eyed, blurted out, "Lepers! Lepers!"

"God's teeth!" the guard yelled, as he finally fought off the roosters. "Lepers in the courtyard! I beg thee, run! Open the castle gate!"

Alan a'Dale pushed Amanda behind him, swung his lute around as if it were a weapon to hold back a fire-breathing dragon. "I shall protect thee, my muse!"

Treena nudged Amanda. "Like I said, restraining order."

Drake rubbed his eyes. "Is—is that Jordan and Ravi? They look like something right outta the *Night of the Living Dead* movie."

Amanda peered around Alan a'Dale. Drake was right. The boys were made up as if they were zombie wannabes. Both wore black robes with stitched-on white patches and tall red hats, while their faces looked like they'd been through a meat grinder. Strings of shredded, bloodied skin hung off their cheeks, and in their scab-covered hands they clutched a set of batons with carved forks on the ends. She grimaced. This was definitely Ravi's handiwork.

She lightly touched Alan a'Dale's shoulder. "It's okay. They're my friends. They're not really lepers."

"Dost thou jest? My eyes see only lepers."

"Your eyes saw a hunchback too, Alan," Amanda whispered.

The sharp sound of wood banging together drew Amanda back to Ravi and Jordan. They were both furiously banging their batons together like inefficient fly swatters.

"Why are they doing that, Alan?"

"Lepers bang their clappers together as a warning for those not stricken," he replied.

"You guys sure know how to clear a room!" Drake shouted. "And all along I thought only Treena's acting could do that!"

"Zounds, Jordan, Ravi, I thought I told thee to stay in Much's cart!" Jean la Nailor shouted, running toward them. "Dost thou ever listen?"

"Do you see a cart anywhere, la Nailor?" Jordan asked, banging away.

Robyn Hodekin and Melody Spencer followed in Jean's gigantic footsteps. Tuck was close behind, wagging his tail and chomping down on a fish he'd found. Smoke from fires curled and curdled, making it hard for Amanda to survey the grounds. She squinted, but couldn't find Miriam anywhere.

"Melody!" Amanda yelled, waving. "Over here!"

Melody turned, her mouth opened. She directed Robyn and Jean to go help Jordan and Ravi. Tuck lobbed after the two boys, while she dashed over to Amanda, Treena, and Drake. She gathered them in her arms and hugged them fiercely. Amanda felt the strength of her squeeze, her reassuring embrace, warm her insides like a home-cooked meal.

"We missed you too, Melody," Drake grunted.

"Drake, FYI—you're grabbing my butt," Treena said, grimacing.

Melody released them and looked around. "Where's Professor Lucas?"

Amanda eyed Drake and Treena. "Sheriff Crowley ordered him to be taken to the deepest cavern. That's all we know."

Melody frowned. "Sheriff Crowley? Professor Crowley is here?"

"Yeah, and he's one bad dude, Melody," Drake replied. "He took Treena's and my Babel necklaces then left us to be tortured in the dungeon. If it wasn't for Amanda and Miriam—"

"Miriam? Maid Miriam?"

"The one and only," Treena said. "But if you ask me the girl needs some serious anger management sessions."

The sound of the crowd had taken on a rougher, nastier tone. Some people had hung back and gathered up whatever they could find lying on the ground—vegetables, fish or fruits seemed to be their favorites. They started pelting Jordan and Ravi, shrieking and cursing at them to leave. Tuck growled, baring his teeth, while Jordan used his clappers like a ping pong racket, deflecting anything that headed his way. Ravi seemed to be having the time of his life, banging and scaring everyone silly, until half a rotten cabbage hit him in the face. Jean and Robyn worked together to divert the mob, but so far, they weren't having any luck. The people even turned on them, and they started to get pummeled. Tuck whined and dug himself under a pile of flour sacks.

"What's with Jordan and Ravi's *Dawn of the Dead* look?" Treena asked.

"It was Ravi's brilliant idea," Melody replied, pushing a dark tendril away from her face. "He had a gel wound kit stashed in his backpack, and thought it would be a wonderful diversion to scare people away while we all escaped in Much's father's bread cart. I suppose we'll have to come up with another plan."

"Okay, new plan, new diversion," Amanda said. "Any suggestions?"

"Dost my muse wish me to help her?" Alan a'Dale asked, placing his hands on Amanda's shoulders.

"Who's he?" Melody asked, warily.

Drake stifled a laugh. "Her new BFF."

Amanda's cheeks flamed. "Um, Melody, this is Alan a'Dale. He was imprisoned in the dungeon with Drake and Treena."

"Milady Melody," Alan a'Dale said, bowing.

Melody furrowed her brow. "Alan a'Dale? The minstrel?"

"Nay, milady Melody, a jongleur." His pride was evident in his stance.

"What's the difference between a minstrel and a jongleur?"

Alan a'Dale beamed as if he were being asked to go to Disneyland. He searched the grounds as the shadows were starting to eat away the light, then strutted toward an abandoned fire away from the crowd. He snatched up three thick sticks from the pit, each with an end ablaze, and began to throw the torches up in the air—one by one—as if he were part of a circus act. Walking back over like this was the most normal thing, Alan a'Dale balanced a glowing stick on his forehead, while keeping the other two blazing batons in the air.

"Great impression of a birthday candle." Treena clapped.

"Yeah, if he knew you were coming he'd have baked a cake," Drake laughed.

Alan a'Dale continued with his juggling act, keeping the flaming sticks in the air, while walking closer to where the four boys were getting splattered with fruit and veggies. Spying an unhitched wagon full of straw parked behind the abusive mob, the wandering jongleur threw not one, but two torches into the wagon. *Whoosh,* went the straw as the hungry fire ate it up—*sizzle, snap, crack*—its fiery tongues licking away at the wagon as if it were the main course. Half the people disbursed, fleeing toward the opening castle gate to escape. Next, Alan a'Dale took his last burning stick and lit a line of grain to separate them from the rest of the crowd.

Suddenly, Much the Miller's son, now red-faced, huffing, and sweating, drove up in his cart. It looked scraped and beaten along one side, but at least it was upright. The lathered gray horses whinnied and stamped, warning the people to get out of their way. Jordan and Ravi hopped in the back first, followed by Robyn, Jean, and Tuck—his tail now up between his legs.

That's our cue. Amanda grabbed Drake and Treena by the arms, and pulled them toward the cart.

"Come on, Melody!" Amanda yelled behind her. "Next stop, Sherwood Forest!"

"Right behind you, Amanda!" Melody replied, scooping up a satchel of round bread that had been thrown from Much's cart.

Drake squirmed. "Ouch! Stop twisting my arm, Amanda!"

Amanda grunted. "Would you rather be twisted like a pretzel on the rack?"

"Good point," Drake muttered. He headed for the cart and jumped in.

Treena bent down to snatch a set of bells left behind by one of the minstrels before she followed Drake into the back of the cart. Alan a'Dale gently lifted Amanda and Melody in before he boarded. They were good to go. Amanda scanned the area one more time in search of Miriam, but it was useless—it was too dark, smoky, and noisy.

"W-Where's my uncle?" Jordan asked, his eyes darting around.

Amanda gulped, then reached over to pat his shoulder. It felt slimy and gross. "It's a long story, Jordan. He's alive. That's all you need to know for now."

Just as they passed through the castle gate, Treena quickly pulled on Jordan's big sweatshirt over her backpack and started ringing the bells she'd scored off the ground.

"Sanctuary!" she yelled in a low, somber voice. "Sanctuary!"

13. A Band of Merry Teens

"**M**mmm, thiss shure hiths the spot, Melody," Treena said with her mouth full of bread.

"Ditto," Drake said, dipping his fingers into his bread bowl full of stew. "How'd you learn to cook over a fire, Melody?"

"My father used to take me on camping trips," Melody replied wistfully. "He was quite the stickler for living off the land. Often he'd trap a rabbit or catch a fish, gather whatever vegetables he could find, and make a wonderful stew out of it. Now that I think of it, I'm glad I paid attention."

"Me too," Amanda said. "Good thing you nabbed the sack of bread. I'm so hungry, I could eat a horse." She stopped and looked at Melody. "BTW—what kind of meat did you use in this?"

Melody giggled. "Not to worry, Amanda, Robyn supplied the rabbit, fresh out of the forest. Besides, it's forbidden by the church to eat horse meat in these times."

Smiling, Amanda picked out a deformed carrot from her bread bowl. It turned to mush as soon as it touched her tongue, and she savored the strong flavor as it slid down her throat. She felt something solid nudge her knee. She looked down. With big, brown eyes, Tuck stared up at her, drooling and begging for a scrap of food. She ignored him, so he pawed her foot, his thick sharp nails digging into her skin. Amanda opened her mouth to scold him and her nose flared. He smelled like a wet blanket in a fish market. Tuck nudged Amanda again, this time with more urgency. She sighed, then gave in and tossed the remnants of her bread bowl to him.

"Not hungry?" Jean le Nailor asked, prodding Jordan with his staff.

Jordan looked up and shrugged. "No. Here, Jean, you have it."

Amanda peered over Jordan's shoulder. He had barely touched the stew that Melody had prepared earlier and had left to season over the fire pit in Robyn's cave.

"Zounds, Jordan, dost thou know how many go without food around us?" Jean asked.

"Don't know, don't care," Jordan mumbled, his vacant eyes staring into the fire.

Amanda could tell Jordan wasn't up for a lecture. All he cared about was getting his uncle back from Crowley in one safe piece. She shivered. The cave they were hiding in, Robyn's hideout, was damp and cramped. The air was heavy with smoke. Night had devoured the sun, and a half moon now hung in the sky, her silvery rays peering through the darkened foliage like an ethereal voyeur.

Melody gently nudged Jordan's arm. "Eat, Jordan. You'll need your strength for tomorrow."

"Why? What's so special about tomorrow?" Jordan asked, gazing at the popping embers.

"FYI—it's May Day, or rather D-Day, for us," Amanda whispered. She had to be careful what she said because lover-boy—a.k.a. Alan a'Dale—was seated on her other side. "We have to solve the Timekeeper riddle by tomorrow if we don't want Belial and Crowley to change history."

"Yeah, and trying not to get killed in the meantime would be a plus," Drake added, as he stoked the fire with more twigs.

"Not helping, Drake," Amanda muttered out of the side of her mouth.

Jordan grunted. "Look, Amanda, we're lost in a time where we don't belong. Where my uncle doesn't belong. How are we supposed to figure out what our mission is when we don't know anything about history? Uncle John's the history wiz, not us."

"I'm with Jordan," Ravi said, wiping cabbage bits out of his ears. "And what if we got caught? Torture? Impalement?

Disembowelment? Don't know about you guys, but I'm not too keen on dying eight hundred years before I'm born."

Amanda rolled her eyes. Sometimes Ravi was more of a drama queen than Treena. She looked around. Alan a'Dale was busy plucking away on his lute, occasionally humming and muttering to himself. Jean had returned to his post at the mouth of the cave, keeping watch, while Robyn and Much had gone off to check on Miriam's whereabouts. Amanda had explained that Miriam helped her get into the castle to rescue her friends, and was somehow left behind in the castle grounds during leper-mania. Robyn, Jean, and Much had also bought the story about Sheriff Crowley using dark witchcraft to take away Treena and Drake's ability to talk sensibly.

"You're not gonna die, Ravi," Amanda said. "We just gotta get with Lilith's program. We gotta learn to look, listen, and trust."

Jordan snorted. He crushed his bread bowl—turnip and carrot guts exploded all over his pants. "You want us to trust Lilith? Take a look around. We should be in a castle, not stuck in a cave. My uncle should be with us, not imprisoned in a cavern. I'd say Lilith has a sick sense of humor if this is her idea of trusting!"

"Take a chill pill, Jordan, and have some faith," Treena said, snapping her fingers. Then she pointed at his bread bowl. "BTW—are you gonna eat that?"

"And speaking of a sick sense of humor," Drake said dryly. "Treena trumps Lilith."

Melody sighed. "Jordan, what Lilith was trying to tell us is we've got to trust enough to know that wherever we step, the path will appear beneath our feet."

"This path sounds way too dangerous for a band of merry teens," Ravi said, shaking his head. "Maybe Robyn or Jean know some adults who could help us rescue Jordan's uncle."

"Adults?" Jean said, joining them by the fire. "Zounds, Ravi, who dost thou think had John Lucas arrested? Truth told, not a child."

Amanda strummed her fingers on her knee. "It's too bad there isn't another way into Nottingham Castle, other than the caves and the gate. No doubt Crowley's got all those entrances covered."

"Yea, there is, milady Amanda," Jean said, leaning against his staff. "Through the cellar caves beneath the Rockyard Inn. 'Tis the truth, these caves lead to the jail."

Amanda's back straightened. "Then the cellar caves are our way back in to rescue Jordan's uncle!"

Jordan rolled his eyes. "And you don't think Crowley's gonna have the whole town of Nottingham on lockdown? We'd be lucky to get out of Sherwood Forest without fingers pointing at us!"

"The only ones Crowley will recognize are Treena and Drake, Jordan," Amanda replied. "He's never seen the rest of us."

"But, Amanda, we'd stick out like scabs on skin," Ravi added.

Treena grimaced. "All of a sudden, I'm not so hungry."

Drake snickered. "Now there's a first."

"I'm afraid Ravi's right," Melody added. "Our clothes, even the way some of us appear, would give us away."

Tuck whined and stuck his nose in the air. He sniffed, then let out a low, welcoming woof. Amanda could hear footsteps approaching the cave. It sounded like *crunch, snap, crunch*, as if someone were walking across hundreds of stalks of celery. Jean la Nailor rushed to the mouth of the cave and whistled. A shrill whistle returned, and as if on cue, Tuck darted out of the cave.

"'Tis Robyn and Much," Jean announced. "I pray they have good news."

Robyn entered the cave. He had a blank look on his face as he pulled off his hood. Much, who carried a torch, followed close behind him. The fire illuminated his puffy face, making it look like a campfire marshmallow.

Robyn nodded to Jean. "The Widow Thatcher told Much that Miriam stopped to help a fallen child running from lepers in the castle grounds. I have sent my coz Wil Scathlocke to the Fitzooth manor to check if she is home safe."

"Oh, I'm sure she's fine, Robyn," Amanda said, hugging her knees. "That girl knows how to defend herself."

Much guffawed. "'Tis the truth, Miriam hath bested many a rogue with 'er bow. 'Tis a shame Sir Robert won't let 'er shoot 'er bow in the archery tourney on May Day."

"Why hath Miriam never told me about sneaking into the castle to bring food to the prisoners?" Robyn asked.

Amanda held up her hand, counting off her fingers. "One, she probably didn't want you worrying, and two, same reason you feed the lepers and make canes for the crippled."

Robyn eyed her strangely. Amanda smiled. "She told me what you do for the stricken and poor of Nottingham. Maybe she wants to help too."

Alan a'Dale strummed his lute. "Hmm, helping the poor and besting a rogue? It sounds like a good gest to me."

"You think this is all a joke, dude?" Jordan growled. Amanda jumped. Jordan flexed his fingers and tightened his hand into a ball. He stood up, his jaw set like a hungry leopard.

"Take it easy, Jordan," Melody said calmly. "Alan's talking about a 'gest' with a G. It's a long poem that tells a story."

"I wish I knew what was going on," Treena muttered to Drake. "It's like going to a movie then having to get up, go out, come back in, get up, go out, come back in, over and over again."

Drake grunted. "Yeah, or figuring out only half of a physics equation."

Treena wrinkled her brow. "You're kidding, right?"

"You're both not missing much," Amanda said, standing. "Miriam's still unaccounted for, Robyn's worried, Alan's trying to be creative, and Jordan's being a gigantic douche."

Jordan growled and pushed her. Amanda put on her warrior face and pushed back. Jordan clenched his teeth and pushed her harder. Stumbling two steps back, Amanda grounded herself, and just as she was about to throw her weight into it, Melody stepped between her and Jordan.

"That's quite enough, you two!" she yelled, wagging a finger.

Tuck whimpered and crawled behind Treena. Melody shot Amanda a warning look and then turned her attention to Jordan. "I know you're angry, Jordan, but this sort of attitude is not helping anyone, especially your uncle. We're a team, and we're in this together, whether you like it or not. We'll figure out something, you'll see. My father used to say—"

"Your dad's a knight, Melody! My uncle's just a professor!" Jordan cut in, his nostrils flaring.

Melody stiffened. "What's that supposed to mean?"

Jordan crossed his arms over his chest, and said, "If this happened to your dad instead of my uncle, betcha he'd have a team of knights ready to back him up and break him out. Look around at what I get stuck with for teammates!"

Amanda reached out to touch Melody's shoulder. Melody's body tightened, like an imaginary harness was reining her in. "Jordan's just scared, Melody. Give him some space."

Without saying another word, Melody sighed, sat down on the log, and poked at the fire.

"'Tis true, milady Melody?" Robyn asked, his face half in the shadows as he approached her. "Thy father is a knight?"

Melody looked exhausted, like there was no more fight left in her. She nodded, and said, "Yes, Robyn, but my father has been gone for many years now."

"Killed in the Crusades, milady Melody?" Jean asked softly.

Melody stared blankly into the fire and said, "I truly *wish* that were so, Jean."

Ravi sat upright. His face hardened. "That's a pretty cold-hearted thing to say, Melody," he said a little too boldly.

Melody licked her bottom lip and nodded. "Perhaps it is, Ravi. But at least I would have peace back in my life. At least I would know what happened." Then she hung her head and stared into the fire as if going in a trance. "Twenty years ago my father took my three-year-old daughter on a trip to meet an old family friend in the country. When they failed to show up, I received a frantic message informing me they were missing." Melody's voice suddenly changed, as if she were drowning, fighting to get out the words. "The authorities…were notified. An intensive search…was done. No bodies—" she paused to wipe her eyes and mouth "—or evidence ever turned up."

The only sound Amanda heard was the crackling of the fire. Her shoulders sagged. Ravi was wrong. Melody wasn't cold-hearted. She was broken-hearted. Amanda bent down, wrapped her thin arms around Melody, and gave her a squeeze.

"I'm sorry, Melody," she whispered. "Why didn't you ever tell us?"

Jordan snorted. "News flash, Amanda. Melody never shares anything about her past."

Melody sniffed. "That's because I try not to dwell on my past, Jordan. It…it hurts too much. If…if you'll all excuse me." She broke away from Amanda and hurried out of the cave.

Jean le Nailor started after Melody. Before Jean disappeared into the darkness, he yelled out, "Fear not, Robyn, I will watch over her."

Amanda clenched her teeth. "Oh, that's great, Jockstrap! You're about as sensitive as a rhino's butt."

"I'll second that," Drake said. "That was unsportsmanlike conduct, Jordan."

"Yeah, and I'll third it," Treena added. "Ravi can join you in the time-out chair."

Ravi wiped his mouth. "Sorry, it's just that when Melody said she wished her father had been killed, she sounded cold and closed-up, like my father did on the day I crushed my hand in his stupid machine. All I was trying to do was help him by removing a pail that got stuck, but instead, he freaked and made me feel worthless, useless, like it was my fault."

Treena nudged Ravi. "It was never your fault, Ravi. Maybe your dad was just scared. Besides, it's nothing that a little one-on-one therapy won't fix."

"Yeah, Ravi, you can probably use Treena's shrink," Drake said, grinning.

Jordan raked his hand through his damp hair. He took a deep breath in, then out, as if the bluster had gone out of him. "My bad too, guys. But I didn't think Melody would freak out like she did. I mean, you all gotta admit, she is kind of secretive."

"She may be secretive, but she's honest," Treena said. "Like it or not, she's right—we're a team." Then she put her hand out. "So let's start acting like it."

Jordan placed his hand on top of Treena's. Ravi covered their hands with his prosthesis, followed by Drake, leaving the topper to Amanda. "Goooo Timekeepers!" they yelled together.

Alan a'Dale grunted. "Must thou yell? I'm composing a ballad for the morrow to sing for the good people of Nottingham."

"But, Alan, aren't you afraid of getting caught again?" Amanda asked.

He chuckled lightly. "Nay, my muse, I shall hide amongst the minstrels, jongleurs, fencers, and jesters wandering the streets. Too much merriment and mischief will be going on for the guards to bother with a rogue like me."

Alan a'Dale resumed strumming and plucking on his lute, playing with words and metaphors and rhymes the way Amanda did when she composed a poem. The sound of lowered voices drifted to Amanda. She looked behind her. Robyn had led Much to the back of the cave. The odd word filtered to her. She made out *Miriam not acting like 'erself,* from Much, and *'Tis most odd,* from Robyn. But that was all she could hear.

"What does the Timekeepers' log say again?" Drake asked. "Maybe it will give us a clue."

Amanda sighed as she pulled out the log. She unlocked the clasp, flipped to where she had last written, and whispered, *"Games and songs and revelry, act as the cloak of devilry. So that an English legend may give to the poor, we must travel to Nottingham to even the score."*

Jordan rubbed his jaw thoughtfully. "Okay, guys, time for a huddle. Let's do the five Ws. We've already figured out *who* we're supposed help—the legendary Robin Hood. *Where* we are— Nottingham, and *when* our mission is supposed to happen—May 1st, 1214. So now we gotta figure out *why* we're here, and *what* we need to do to get back home."

"You forgot the big H, Jordan," Treena said. *"How* do we stop time from changing?"

"The *cloak of devilry*," Ravi muttered. "Sounds like something evil or diabolic."

"Whoa, wait, I think I've got a dictionary stashed at the bottom of my backpack," Treena said, rummaging through it. A small tube fell out as she pulled out a ratty old paperback.

"What's this?" Ravi asked, picking up the tube and examining it.

Treena snatched it back. "Er, a tube of hair tint."

Jordan looked at her sideways. "Hair tint?"

She shrugged. "In case I need to do a touch up for an audition, silly."

"Here, gimme the dictionary, Treena," Drake said. He flipped through it quickly. "Hmm, *devilry* can also mean malicious fun or mischief."

"It's like putting a jig-saw puzzle together with words," Treena said, puffing her cheeks.

Amanda's eyes widened. "Wait—merriment and mischief— that's it!" She whirled around. "Alan?"

Startled, Alan a'Dale plinked on his lute when he should have plunked. He sighed and looked up at Amanda. "What now, muse?"

Amanda batted her eyelashes and plastered on the best Cheshire cat smile she could muster. "Your muse *needs* you."

14. *The Bow of a Legend*

*I*t was by far the worst night of Amanda Sault's life. Between Jordan's snores, Ravi's nightmares, Treena's grumbling stomach, Drake talking in his sleep, and Tuck's frequent farts, Amanda was lucky to get an hour's sleep. She shivered as she pushed herself off the straw bed Much had made for them. The fire had burned down into embers and a small pot of what looked like oatmeal hung over it.

She glanced around. Robyn, Much, and Jean were nowhere to be seen, and Alan a'Dale had not returned since Amanda had sent him on her own personal mission. If the Timekeepers were going to be "the cloak of devilry" then they'd best act and dress the part. And how better to do that than to blend in with a crowd of mischief-making medieval entertainers? Since Alan knew many of the minstrels and performers, he'd been appointed to scrounge up some instruments and clothes that would conceal their twenty-first century identities from Crowley and his cronies. Of course their mission had deviated when Professor Lucas was taken hostage, making him the number one priority.

Amanda yawned, scooped a finger's portion of oatmeal, and walked out of the cave. She popped the ball of oatmeal into her mouth while scanning the forest. Through the leaves, the rising sun sparkled its greeting. The air was still heavy with moisture, and everything about the forest seemed fresh to her. Fresh and pure and vibrant. She inhaled deeply, grateful her allergies hadn't hung around to haunt her.

A cracking noise startled her. Now on alert, she scanned the area and found Melody Spencer sitting on a rock. Apparently oblivious to everything around her, Melody leaned against a long, thin branch, her expression as stoic as ever. Jean le Nailor's cape was draped over her shoulders.

Amanda stood in silence and observed her. Why hadn't Melody come back to the cave last night? Was she mad at them? Or was Melody ashamed of her past? Amanda sighed, gathering the nerve to go talk to her. As she quietly padded through the forest path, the branch in Melody's hands suddenly bent. In that moment, a ray of light landed on the branch and illuminated it, making it look like a sideways rainbow. Amanda froze. Her heart began to pulsate in fast, direct beats. She knew. She now knew why they were here and what they had to do.

"That's it!" Amanda yelled triumphantly.

Startled, Melody let go of the branch, lost her balance, and fell from her perch. Jean's cape tumbled from her shoulders.

Amanda raced toward her. "Melody! Are you okay?"

Stunned, Melody gave her head a shake. "I…I think so, Amanda. What's all the shouting about?"

Amanda helped Melody to her feet, then picked up the branch and shook it. "This is it! The answer to why we're here and what we have to do!"

"A yew branch is the answer?" Melody asked, while retrieving Jean's sloughed-off cape. She shook it out, folded it, and laid it across the rock.

Amanda nodded.

Melody stared at her blankly, like she didn't get it. Maybe she didn't. Amanda laughed, threw her arms around Melody, and looked her in the eyes. "Doncha see, Melody? When I watched you leaning against this branch, it resembled a longbow to me, and that's when I got the connection. In our time, Robin Hood is known for using a longbow, not a crossbow."

Melody's lips curled. Amanda grinned. It was nice to see her smile again.

"By George, I think you've got it, Amanda," Melody said, hugging her tightly.

Never mind George. It was enough to get Melody back on track. Amanda returned the hug and said, "Sorry 'bout last night, Melody. You know, what happened and stuff."

At first, Melody stiffened, and then she relaxed as if letting something heavy inside fall away. She inhaled deeply. "You don't have to apologize to me, Amanda. It's nothing you or Jordan or Ravi said, it's just that...that I feel so empty at times. In truth, I guess I keep trying to fill an endless void in my life."

"Whatcha mean, Melody?"

She sighed. "Since my family disappeared, I've thrown myself into my father's work, as if living for him, trying to keep part of him alive. Papa was a gifted doctor, a pioneer in the way he treated his patients. He believed in treating a person as a whole entity, not just the body, and realized the energy that surrounds us, that makes us up, is dependent upon our very thoughts, attitudes, beliefs, and even our environment. Most called him a fool, but some thought him a genius. With support from a handful of influential friends, Spencer Wellness Clinics began to thrive in certain areas of England and Europe. He gave many people a reason to live again. I am very proud to be a part of my father's dream."

"What about *your* dreams, Melody? Doncha have any?"

Melody gazed out into the forest. "I wanted to be a ballet dancer, but Papa thought it best I should learn to fence instead. That's how I met Bernard Hamilton. At first he was my teacher, and then as time went on, I fell in love with him." Melody paused, dropped her chin to her chest. "We parted ways the day our daughter was born. Bernard decided to choose fencing over family."

Melody snorted then. Something she rarely did.

Intrigued, Amanda sat on the rock, and leaned against the branch. "What's your daughter's name?"

"Brenna. Brenna Kathleen Spencer," Melody whispered.

"That's a pretty name. Did Brenna like to dance too?"

Melody stared out into the forest again, as if it was magically pulling her into the past. She grazed her bottom lip with her teeth. "Yes. Brenna had quite the imagination when it came to dancing. It didn't matter where we were or who was there, Brenna just let loose and danced up a storm. She never stuffed her feelings."

Stuffed feelings? Amanda could relate to that. She had a folder full of feelings on what she wanted to say to her mother. But she never found the guts to open her mouth. Instead, she used her poetry to help get the gunk out. Then, it dawned on her that she and Melody weren't so different after all, and she had something to say that might help "fill her up".

"I bet you were a great mom, Melody."

"Thank you, Amanda," Melody replied in a broken voice. She kissed Amanda's cheek.

An intense sensation of warmth raced through Amanda's whole body. She embraced this feeling, not wanting it to pass, but knowing she couldn't hold onto it either. She gripped the yew branch as if it were a staff in order to ground her, steady her. It felt strong in her hands—perfect for the bow of a legend.

Smiling, Amanda jumped off the rock. "Last night, Much mentioned something about an archery tournament being held on May Day. If we can get Robyn to change and use a longbow, maybe he could win. That way everything ever written about Robin Hood won't be erased."

Melody thumbed her chin. "Yes, that makes sense, Amanda. Even if some of the historical texts aren't factual, the truth behind the legend would continue to survive."

"Good. So how do we go about making a bow?"

Melody smiled. She dipped into a deep skirt pocket and pulled out a small roll of gardening twine and a Swiss Army knife. She motioned Amanda to hand over the branch and together they bent it so that it formed a perfect bow. Melody quickly tied the twine to both ends and then flipped the knife open to cut away the excess twine. With an eye for precision, she started to carve out the bow's handle where an arrow would rest. She followed the grain of the wood like a river furrowing into the earth. It wouldn't be a fancy-looking bow, but it would definitely do the trick. Melody held up the bow, checking it once, twice, three times over before giving it her nod of approval.

"Mmm. We'll have to make some arrows as well, Amanda. The crossbow bolts are too short for a longbow."

"Sure, but how do we go about converting Robyn from the crossbow to the longbow?"

Melody never got a chance to answer. An arrow whistled through the bushes, buzzed directly between them, and struck the boulder they had sat on. It splintered upon impact. Amanda held her breath. That was close. Two people emerged from the thicket—Robyn and Much, who was breathing heavily. Amanda exhaled, releasing a sloppy fizzle sound. Robyn's eyes darted over them as if he were at a tennis match, then turned to Much, took away his crossbow, and slapped him across the back of the head.

"Stupid simpkin! How many times have I told thee that anyone can shoot a crossbow? 'Tis so simple, even a child can use one!"

Much hung his head. "Sorry, Robyn," he mumbled.

"I beg thy pardon, milady Melody, milady Amanda," Robyn said. "Art thou hurt?"

"No. I'm good," Amanda said, wiping spittle from the side of her mouth.

"Yes, we're quite fine, Robyn," Melody said. "No harm done. Has your cousin Wil brought you any news of Miriam?"

Robyn's shoulders slumped. "Nay, milady, Wil hath brought no word."

"Don't worry, Robyn, no news is good news," Melody said reassuringly.

Amanda decided it was show time. "Ever thought about using a longbow, Robyn? After all, Miriam uses one, so how hard can it be?"

"I've been told that a longbow is more accurate for hunting," Melody added.

Robyn screwed up his face as if he had just been asked to eat raw liver.

Much chuckled. "Robyn use a longbow? 'Tis silly to think such things."

Robyn elbowed Much in the gut. "Something amuses thee, simpkin?"

Much rubbed his ample belly and shook his head. "Nay, Robyn, nay, 'tis that thou hast never used a longbow."

"I can think of a couple of good reasons why he should start now," Amanda said.

"Such as?" Robyn asked.

"Well, like you said to Much, *anyone* can shoot a crossbow, but it takes *great skill* to *master* the longbow. And the greater the skill, the higher chance you have to score big with the chicks around Nottingham."

Much puckered his lips. "Why dost thou want Robyn to play with chickens?"

Amanda rolled her eyes. She ignored Much and looked at Robyn. "You know, all the *girls* in Nottingham won't be able to keep their hot little hands off you, once they see you shooting the longbow. Do the math, Robyn—that includes Miriam."

Melody coughed.

Much belched.

Robyn's eyes bugged.

Amanda couldn't believe she had said that. The words just tumbled out of her mouth. It sounded like something Jordan would say. Her cheeks burned. "Uh, wait, what I meant to say was—"

"Teach me!" Robyn blurted, tossing the crossbow aside.

"Huh? What?"

"He wants you and your hot little hands to teach him, Amanda," Melody said, grinning as she passed off the longbow to her.

Amanda gulped. She knew nothing about archery. Great. Now what? Amanda looked at the longbow, then glanced at Melody. Melody's grin had turned into a blatant smirk. What was up with that?

Before Amanda had time to ask her, Melody turned to Robyn and started counting on her fingers. "We'll need some ash branches, as many goose feathers as you can find, some sinew and flint to make arrows, as well as a couple of bales of hay for targets. Wake the others if you need their help. How fast can you get us these things, Robyn?"

Robyn stumbled, bowed before Melody, then grabbed Much by the arm and spun him around like a top. "Thou heardest milady Melody! Get on with thee, Much!"

Amanda watched with her mouth agape as the boys ripped through the forest like a pair of flying arrows. Melody poked her from behind. She turned; Melody was still grinning.

Amanda furrowed her brow. "Don't tell me you know something about archery."

"All right, I won't."

"How come you never said anything when Treena brought it up yesterday?"

"Have you forgotten, Amanda? Lilith told us to *pay attention* first, and then *act*. Well, before I took up fencing, I dabbled a bit in archery."

Amanda giggled. "The way I see it, you would have made a better actor than a dancer!"

Three hours later, Amanda figured that "dabbled" was an understatement. In the short time she had known her, Amanda had learned that Melody tended to immerse herself into the things that interested her. Whether it was gardening, landscaping, cooking, volunteering, or nursing cuts and bruises, Melody took it to heart. Archery was no exception. Even Robyn seemed impressed.

Two bales of hay were set up in the meadow by Much, each strategically positioned by counting off a number of strides. Jordan and Drake were back at the cave, helping Much and Jean make arrows, while Treena and Ravi had decided to put their theatrical creativity to good use by volunteering to help Alan a'Dale prepare what was needed for them to pass as medieval performers.

Amanda watched Robyn shoot his arrow. She smiled. Yup, he was getting the hang of it.

"How is that shot, milady Melody?" Robyn shouted.

Melody sprinted toward the first round hay bale. She skidded to a stop and checked the position of the arrow. She gave him the thumbs up sign.

Robyn looked at Amanda oddly. She laughed. "Melody says you're doing better."

Robyn sighed. "Truth be told, 'tis hard to adjust to the longbow."

"You'll get used to it, Robyn. It just takes practice," she encouraged him..

Robyn's eyes lit up. "Dost thou think so, milady Amanda?"

Amanda nodded. "Face it, Robyn, you're a natural. Melody only gave you the basics on how to hold the bow and where to plant your feet. The rest of what you already knew just fell into place."

Robyn blushed. In fact, he almost turned the same color as his hair.

"So…do you think you'll be ready for the archery tournament this afternoon?" She asked.

Robyn dropped his bow. "Archery tournament? Dost thou jest, milady Amanda?"

Jest? No, she wasn't joking. Was Robyn? Surely not. Amanda crossed her arms over her chest. "The whole point of changing you over to the longbow was so that you could enter the archery contest in Nottingham today and win. No problemo."

"Yea, problemo! Sir Guy of Gisborne will be there. He is older and an expert archer. He always wins. I have no chance against him! If that is thy plan for me, this ends now!"

Robyn kicked his bow aside and stomped off.

"Anything wrong, Amanda?" Melody shouted across the meadow.

Nope. Nothing I can't handle. Amanda waved, grinned, and nodded. "Fine. Everything's fine!" she shouted back.

She took a deep breath. It was time to channel her inner warrior. Amanda wasn't going to let this medieval douche's low self-esteem get to her. Robyn was going to be in that contest whether he liked it or not. Time—his time—depended on it. She bolted after him with a force she'd never experienced before and hit her target harder than an arrow.

Amanda and Robyn tumbled over each other and landed short of a babbling brook. Her braid came loose, making her dark brown hair cling to the sides of her face like a bearded lady in a freak show. She grabbed Robyn's green hood, inched his face closer to hers and glared.

Robyn howled with laughter.

"What's so funny, Hodekin?"

"Thou racest like a man, thou hittest hard like a man, and now thou lookest like a man."

Amanda grunted. She released Robyn and rolled off of him. "Sorry, Robyn," she muttered. "I guess I lost it."

He stopped laughing. "Lost what, milady?" He looked around the grass.

She wanted to say *dignity*, but didn't. "Never mind."

"I promise, 'twas not to insult thee, milady. Thou remindest me of Miriam, 'tis all."

Amanda brushed the hair out of her face. "You really like Miriam, don't you?"

Robyn's face shined. "Aye. It frets me so to wonder why Miriam hath not been acting like herself lately." His chin hit his chest. "I suppose Miriam Fitzooth deserves better. I have no title to my name or money in my purse."

"You would if you won the archery contest, Robyn. Think about it. You win the title of best archer, you're awarded money, and you go buy a big estate somewhere in the country. Tell me what girl wouldn't want that?"

He chuckled. "Such strange talk. But thou hast given me much to think about, milady. I thank thee."

Without warning, Robyn grasped Amanda's hand and planted a gentle kiss on it. This made her body hum. *So much for chivalry being dead.* Amanda sensed a blush rising up her neck about the same time she caught a movement in the bushes. Startled, she scanned the area and saw what looked like the outline of a person running away. Her heart clenched and she inhaled sharply. Someone had been watching them.

15. A Helping Hand

"*T*ouch my face once more, Sharma, and I swear, I'll—"
Jordan never had a chance to finish. Ravi covered his lips with woad—the thick blue face paint Alan a'Dale had collected from his minstrel friends. Alan also managed to score a few bells to use as instruments, a couple of swords, some colorful capes and woolen tunics, and one jester's outfit consisting of pointy boots, a blue and white tunic, and a jiggling donkey-eared hat. The jester's costume fit Jordan perfectly, making him the obvious choice to wear it. Amanda couldn't help herself. She started to laugh.

"Don't move, Jordan. You want to look like a real jester, don't you?" Ravi asked.

Amanda would bet Jordan's entire baseball card collection that he didn't.

"Okay, that's it," Ravi said approvingly. "Half your face is painted. You're ready."

Jordan scowled at him. "Yeah, ready to puke all over you."

Ravi rolled his eyes. "Stop being a suck. It's like the stuff the makeup artists used in the movie *Braveheart*. I happen to think it looks wicked." He prodded Jordan's cheek.

Treena giggled as she pulled on a yellow tunic. "He looks more like 'Foolheart' to me."

Drake snickered while struggling into a red tunic too big for him. "Yeah, minus the kilt."

Jordan grunted and smacked Ravi's hand away. "How come I couldn't be something cooler, like a fencer or juggler?"

"Do you know how to fence like Melody or juggle like Alan?" Amanda asked, adjusting the bright green tunic over her shoulders.

Jordan frowned. "No."

She smirked. "And you wonder why you're the fool?"

Amanda picked up two sets of bells and handed them to Treena and Drake. "Since you guys are out of the loop, language-wise, one of you will walk with Ravi and the other with me."

"Can't I go with Melody?" Drake asked.

"She'll be doing a fencing routine with Robyn," Treena said, shaking her bells at him. "So, if you don't wanna get skewered, it's either team Amanda or team Ravi."

"Fine. I'll take Ravi," Drake muttered.

"Did you have to make it sound like I'm your last choice?" Ravi said indignantly.

"Hey, who's gonna walk with me?" Jordan asked, pushing back his fool's cap.

"'Twill be me," Alan a'Dale replied as he sauntered into the cave. He strummed his lute. "Thou shalt mock the crowds, free from their scorn or measure. 'Tis the truth a jester may speak his mind."

"Wait, you mean I get to make fun of people and they can't touch me?" Jordan asked. He grinned devilishly. "Sweet!"

Amanda snorted. "And how is that any different from your life back home, Jockstrap?"

"Zounds!" Jean le Nailor said as he entered the cave. "'Tis true what thou hast told me, Much. Jordan makes for a grand jester."

"Aye, Jean, methinks Ravi hath done well," Much said, ambling in behind him.

Tuck loped in after the boys, his enormous brown paws thudding across the dirt floor. His ears went back the moment he saw Jordan. Much gave him a reassuring pat. "'Tis ol' right, Tuck. 'Tis only Jordan. Ravi hath fooled even thee."

Ravi beamed as he tugged on his light blue tunic. "Um, thanks, guys. Now if only Jordan would play the part of a jester and smile more."

"You try smiling with this blue crap on, Sharma."

"Jock-heads have no sense of humor," Ravi said, shaking his head. "I should have covered your whole face and made you look like a Smurf."

Jordan clenched his teeth and took a swipe at Ravi. Jean le Nailor grabbed his hand in mid-air. Jordan tried to pull his hand away. "Let go, la Nailor! I may be shorter than you, but you're *little*, Jean, when it comes to brain matter!"

"Little...Jean?" Much said. Then his face puckered, and he started to laugh hysterically.

Jean released Jordan's hand and turned on Much. "What is so funny, simpkin?"

"*Little Jean*," Much replied while wiping his mouth. "'Tis a grand jest!"

Jean le Nailor jerked. Then he smiled and slapped Much on the back. "Yea, Much, Little Jean doeth me just! 'Tis good for merriment! Jordan is a jester after all."

"Why are they laughing?" Treena asked. "Drake and I are only on half a frequency here."

"Apparently, they seem to like 'Little' Jean's new nickname, compliments of 'Big' Jockstrap," Amanda replied glaring at Jordan.

"Yeah," Ravi added, "either Jordan just changed history or he somehow kept it in sync."

The sound of someone scraping metal against rock made Amanda shiver. She turned toward the mouth of the cave as a scruffy red-headed boy entered. He was about Drake's age, but taller. He dressed like and resembled Robyn, only instead of wearing a green hood and hose, he wore russet. His young face seemed hardened and angry. In one hand he held a fancy silver dagger which he kept sliding across a stone in a quick, almost obsessive manner. Amanda noticed two smaller knives were tucked inside his belt.

"Wil! Thou hast news of Miriam?" Jean asked hopefully.

Wil stopped fiddling with his dagger and looked up at Jean. His fierce, hazel eyes were serious and steady. "Nay, Jean. Sir Robert Fitzooth hath ordered fellow knights to search for her now."

Much groaned. "'Tis bad news."

Wil slowly glanced around the cave. His eyes bugged when he spotted Jordan. "'Tis no time for making merry," he spat.

Suddenly, Jordan laughed like an idiot, moving his head to and fro, making the bells on the tails of his hat jingle excessively. "What do you call a redhead with an attitude?" he asked Wil. Without giving him a chance to answer he said, "Normal."

Much guffawed. Jean laughed.

"Ah, Jordan," Drake muttered. "I think his face is turning redder than his hair."

"More like scarlet," Treena said. "Looks like hues of red on red on red. Talk about clashing your fashion."

Wil growled and lunged for Jordan with his dagger.

"Hey! Back off, you little douche!" Jordan yelled, stumbling backward. "I-I was kidding! I'm Switzerland!"

Before Wil had a chance to reach Jordan, Amanda snatched up Treena's backpack and whacked Wil across the head with it. Stunned, he dropped his dagger, grabbed his head, and fell to his knees.

"Nice role playing, Jordan," Ravi said. "Next time see what happens when you insult someone with a sword."

Amanda tossed the backpack aside, wiped her forehead, and stared down at Wil. "Are...are you crazy, Wil? We're all on the same team! Why would you attack Jordan?"

Wil hung his head. "The knife...speaks for me."

Amanda was taken back. Wil sounded broken and bitter.

"Yon dagger is Wil's justice, milady Amanda," Jean explained. "'Twas taken out of his mother's belly by Wil's own hand not more than a month ago."

Jordan stiffened. "What! Who did—"

"The sheriff's rogues!" Wil cut in, standing. He picked up his knife and stuffed it in his belt with the others.

"But, couldn't you go to the king for justice?" Ravi asked.

"King John appoints the sheriff, Ravi," Jean said. "To do so would go against his royal judgment."

"Well that bites, Jean!" Jordan yelled. "I say it's time we stand together and stick up for the people's rights around Nottingham! Starting now!"

Wil's eyes grew big, and he smiled. He clapped Jordan on the shoulder and said, "Aye, Jordan, 'tis high time!"

Jordan grinned. He turned and started to march out of the cave, but his pointy shoes got caught under a rock. He was down in seconds flat. Laughter filled the cave as Tuck lunged to lick Jordan's face.

Ravi rushed toward Jordan. "No, Tuck! Down! Don't lick the paint off!"

Amanda giggled. "I think you're getting the hang of this jester thing, Jockstrap."

Jordan groaned, then nodded. "BTW—thanks, Amanda, you know, for saving my butt."

Amanda's cheeks grew hot as she heard hurried footsteps behind her.

"Coz!" Robyn shouted, as he set foot in the cave. Then he froze. Wil slowly shook his head. Robyn's whole body slumped, and he strangled the bow in his hand.

"'Tis my fault Miriam is missing," Robyn muttered, his eyes cast down. "I should have stayed in the castle grounds to look for her."

"Maybe Miriam needs some space, Robyn," Amanda said gently. "Much said she wasn't acting like herself lately. Maybe she's got a good reason."

Robyn sighed and looked up. "Aye, 'tis possible Miriam could be helping others I don't know about."

As Ravi struggled to pull Tuck away, Wil helped Jordan up. He nodded his thanks, and then turned toward Robyn. "How's the archery lesson going?"

Robyn gave Jordan an awkward thumbs up sign. "Better."

"Yes, Robyn will be shooting fish in a barrel come this afternoon," Melody added, walking up behind the others.

Robyn looked at Melody strangely. "Why would I want to shoot at fish in a barrel, milady?"

Melody pursed her lips. "Ah, I mean hitting the target."

Amanda giggled. At this rate, if all the Timekeepers kept saying phrases like that, then history would be rewritten for sure.

The streets of Nottingham were muddied and narrow, filled with throngs of chattering people celebrating May Day. A number of houses—all made of timber coated with a gray muck and thick thatched roofs—stood at odd angles from the road, like a subdivision gone awry. The noise of bleating sheep, hogs bawling, peddlers shouting, people haggling, and babies crying sounded chaotic to Amanda, like a Lollapalooza concert in full swing.

Melody and Robyn led the way and looked like they were having fun showing their skills with the swords. A long hooded Lincoln-green cape covered Melody from head to toe and swirled around her ankles like chasing leaves every time she parried and lunged. Amanda hoped they would pass for thirteenth-century entertainers, even as the *clink, clink, clink* sound of their swordplay grated on her nerves.

Laughter and singing filled Amanda's ears as she shook her bells, smiling back at the happy crowd. The aroma of savory cooking teased her. The smell of raw sewage gagged her. Dodging potholes as big as moon craters, Amanda and Treena stuck close together, walking behind Alan a'Dale, Wil, and Jordan. To her right, crowds of people were pushing and grabbing for medieval merchandise on carts.

Treena giggled. "They act like they're shopping for the holidays."

"Some things never change," Amanda muttered.

"How's your face feel, Jordan?" Ravi asked, jiggling his bells behind Jordan.

"Like half of it has had Botox," Jordan replied through a ridiculous grin.

"Keep laughing at the people, Jordan," Alan a'Dale said, as he juggled Wil's three knives in the air. "'Tis expected from a jester."

"Aye, make faces too," Wil added. "Thou must be true."

At Robyn's request, Wil had begrudgingly lent Alan a'Dale his knives while he tagged along ringing the extra set of bells Treena had found in the castle courtyard. Since the town's miller provided most of the grain to brew the ale served at the Rockyard Inn, it was decided that Much, Jean, and Tuck would deliver a wagon full of grain there this morning. Jean had agreed to stash Jordan's, Ravi's, and Treena's backpacks, Robyn's bow and arrows, and Alan a'Dale's lute in the wagon until they met up with them. Amanda guessed that would be soon, seeing as Nottingham castle loomed over them like a ravenous dragon awaiting its dinner.

Alan threw each knife into the air with precision and grace, never once nicking his fingers or drawing blood. People clapped and cheered as he balanced the silver dagger on his nose while throwing the other two knives higher and higher in the air. The melodic garble of medieval flutes and harps and lutes and bells around them worked together in slow-paced harmony and helped Alan keep rhythm with his juggling efforts.

"Uh-oh," Drake muttered, walking beside Treena.

"What's up?" Treena asked, shaking her bells to the tune of a twenty-first-century hit song.

"Soldiers ahead, two o'clock."

Amanda peered around Alan. Drake was right. Thankfully there were only five. "Keep going, keep smiling, and keep ringing your bells," Amanda said. "They won't pay any attention if you don't stick out."

Robyn and Melody moved past the soldiers easily, attacking and counter-attacking each other to the ohhs and ahhs of the people. Even a couple of the soldiers cheered them on. Some richly dressed merchants threw money at their feet, which Robyn gladly scooped up as he bowed to them. Just ahead of Melody and Robyn, an overloaded wagon was stuck in a pothole. It blocked the street. Two men were trying desperately to push the wagon out, yet didn't seem to want to get too close to it. As Amanda got nearer, she found out why. The wagon was full of manure and sewage. She puckered her mouth and plugged her nose.

"Whew! Ravi is that you?" Treena asked.

"I was just about to ask you the same thing," Ravi replied.

"Ohh, that's nasty," Drake added, grimacing.

Treena giggled. "No. That's evil. Med-evil. Get it?"

"Rogue!" a hawk-nosed soldier yelled, as he pointed at Alan a'Dale. "Yon silver dagger, 'tis mine!"

Amanda stopped. So did the others. Alan was balancing Wil's silver knife on his forehead. He ceased juggling and glanced at the soldier. Wil stood in the middle of the street, open-mouthed and still as a statue. His face flashed to scarlet. Jordan jumped to Alan's side, laughing and joking, shaking his head, ringing the bells, but was pushed roughly away by one of the soldiers.

"Why, sirrah, 'tis but a silver dagger," Alan said in a jovial manner. "What makes thee think 'tis thy knife?"

The soldier sneered. Amanda could see most of his teeth were missing or rotting. He spit on the ground near Alan's feet. "The last time I laid me eyes on it, 'twas in a wench's belly for not paying 'er taxes."

The other soldiers with him chortled like animals being slaughtered.

Wil was trembling now. He placed his hands together as if saying a prayer.

Jordan stiffened. He balled his fists. Uh-oh. This wasn't good. Amanda poked Ravi and whispered, "Red alert. Get Jordan away from that soldier before he does something stupid."

Ravi nodded. He raced over and grabbed Jordan's shoulder. Without turning, Jordan shrugged off Ravi's hand. But Ravi didn't budge. Growling, Jordan reached over, grasped his hand, and tugged hard. It suddenly popped off Ravi's arm and started slapping Jordan in the face.

Jordan twisted around to find Ravi with his mouth agape, staring at his stump. The crowd started roaring with laughter and clapped while Ravi's prosthesis stopped its assault to cling to Jordan's face using its kung fu grip.

Drake's eyes bugged. "Did...did you guys know Ravi could do that?"

Treena shook her head. "No. But from now on, I'm gonna be extra careful when I ask Ravi to give me a helping hand."

"OMG—they must think this is all part of an act," Amanda said.

Jordan managed to pry off the assaulting appendage and threw it at the hawk-nosed soldier. "Sic'em, Sharma!" he yelled.

The soldier's eyes widened as Ravi's hand started to give him a smack-down. It punched him in the nose and gouged him in the eyes like a corny *Three Stooges* repeat. The other soldiers were bent over laughing hysterically.

Wil's face changed from red to pink, and his mouth formed the biggest jack-o-lantern smile Amanda had ever seen. He crossed himself at least a dozen times.

"'Tis witchcraft?" Alan a'Dale asked, backing away.

Jordan flashed him a mischievous grin. "Nope. It's Ravi-craft!"

"Get my hand back, Jensen!" Ravi yelled, coddling his handless arm. "Now!"

The soldier was now down on his knees, screaming and trying to pry off the prosthesis. Jordan wrapped both hands around it and pulled as if he were in a tug-of-war contest. Ravi's hand released the soldier's bloodied face, and Jordan sailed backward into Ravi, who flew back into Drake, knocking the bells out of his hands and the hood off his head. Amanda flinched as she heard the *whump* of their landing. All around them, the people were going crazy with laughter, cheers, and whistles.

Jordan quickly flipped Ravi his prosthesis. He smiled. "Next time, keep your hands to yourself, Sharma."

"Sorry, Jordan, I didn't know my hand could *do* that. It's still all new to me. All I know is that I was *thinking* I had to stop you, and for some reason my hand switched to auto pilot—like it had a *mind* of its own."

Drake groaned, rubbing the back of his head. "Maybe that crystal Lilith put in your hand is hardwired to what you're feeling and thinking, Ravi. Maybe it's supposed to give you some kind of superpower."

Ravi's face beamed. "You think so?"

"It's the only thing that makes sense," Amanda added as she helped Drake up.

Ravi grinned as he placed his prosthesis back into position. He wiggled all his fingers, making sure they still worked. "Super power, eh? I could get to like this."

Jordan stood up and gently probed his face. "I'm not so sure I could."

"'Tis the escaped poacher!" a soldier yelled from across the street. He drew his sword and pointed it at Drake. "The sheriff will pay handsomely for 'im!"

"Uh-oh, busted," Treena said, moaning. "That's one of the soldiers who caught us in Sherwood Forest yesterday."

"In the name of King John, thou rogues art under arrest," another soldier yelled as he charged them.

16. Going Beneath the Surface

"*En garde*, rogue!" Melody yelled as she cracked her blade hard against the advancing soldier's scrawny butt. He tripped up and fell, face first, into a mud puddle.

Robyn joined Melody. He took care of the second soldier by whacking the sword out of his hand and slicing a huge hole in the back of his hose. In a panic, the soldier tried to cover his exposed hairy cheeks and tripped over the other fallen soldier.

"All for one!" Melody cheered, clanking swords with Robyn.

The crowd burst into applause and cheers.

Amanda spied more soldiers, all gangly and vulgar, rushing toward them from behind. They laughed and drooled like a pack of wild hyenas. She gulped. Their only hope was to outrun them by going around the wagon stuck in the middle of the road up ahead. The soldier whose face had done a slam-dance with Ravi's prosthesis drew his sword and attacked Melody. She counter-attacked as if she were a lioness protecting her pride.

"'Tis time to bid farewell," Alan a'Dale announced. He rammed the silver dagger's hilt into the skull of its former owner, knocking him out cold. "Penance...for Wil."

"Take that, you douche-bag!" Jordan yelled. "Boom!"

Wil fell to his knees. "I thank thee, Jordan, Alan. My mother hath been honored."

"Like Amanda said, we're on the same team, Wil," Jordan replied, helping him up.

Melody curtsied. "And thank you, Alan."

Alan a'Dale bowed. "'Tis my pleasure, milady."

"Do you guys think you can stop with playing nice now?" Amanda asked. "We've gotta get to the Rockyard Inn before those soldiers reach us."

"Aye, milady Amanda is right," Robyn said, waving his sword in the air. "Let us take our leave."

Amanda caught Treena waving at the people, throwing imaginary kisses to them as if they were at a red carpet event. She grabbed Treena's hood and dragged her up the road. "If you ever want to see your star on the sidewalk, I suggest you move!"

"Okay, okay," Treena said in a huff. "I was only connecting with my fans."

The men, women, and children lined on the side of the road whistled, cheered, and clapped as they passed them. Mud caked Amanda's sandals as she darted toward the sideways wagon. She covered her mouth as soon as they got within twenty feet of it. The air was rank, rancid, and offensive, like stepping into an overflowing outhouse. A couple of men were trying to pry the wagon's wheel out of the pothole using a pole, but it didn't budge. In a fit of pique, the bigger of the two men threw the pole on the ground and stomped away. Robyn reached the wagon first, and using his sword, cut the bottom latch on the back gate.

"Cut the other latch, milady Melody," Robyn said urgently. "'Twill slow the soldiers!"

Melody raced around, slashed the other latch, and backed away. But nothing happened.

Amanda skidded to a stop, almost banging into Jordan. Holding her breath, she looked up. The back gate had been reinforced with rope at the top to secure its smelly contents from spilling all over the road. Jordan grabbed the pole off the ground and tried to free one of the ropes. Bits of hay and dung dropped on his head.

He grimaced and stepped away. "It's too high, too tight, and too stinky!"

"Hey, wait—couldn't Ravi send his hand up there to loosen those ropes?" Drake asked, straining his neck to look up.

"Yeah, Ravi," Treena added, puffing hard. "Show us your super Boy Scout powers and undo those knots."

Ravi's face scrunched. "Nuh-uh. No way. No how. I've got my hand dirty enough for one day, thank you very much."

Amanda glanced over her shoulder. At least twelve well-armed soldiers were closing in on them. "There's no time, guys. It was a good plan, but we gotta go."

Suddenly, an arrow sliced through the top ropes. Half the gate wrenched and twisted open under the pressure of the dung-hay mixture. Amanda and Jordan jumped back. Some of the smelly contents started to trickle out, but for the most part the gate remained suspended in mid-air, held by a few strands of rope.

"Get thee away from yon wagon, unless, thou wishest to bathe with the soldiers!"

Amanda whirled around. Her eyes widened. "It's Miriam!"

"Miriam?" Robyn cried, turning.

Wil grinned. "Aye! She is safe, Robyn!"

"You heard her, guys! Run!" Jordan yelled.

"Actually, I didn't get the gist of what she said exactly, but—"

"Move already, Treena!" Drake shouted, pushing her out of the way.

Amanda ran to the other side of the wagon to join the others. Miriam slid another arrow out of her belt, took aim, waited until the majority of the soldiers neared the wagon, then let the arrow go. Her arrow sliced through the remaining ropes holding the wagon's gate. Like the force of an erupting volcano, the gate exploded open, allowing for a ton of manure and sewage to spill out of the wagon and pour in an avalanche upon the advancing soldiers.

Miriam jumped down from the pottery vendor's wagon where she'd been positioned. She was wearing the same outfit as yesterday—a green bat-winged dress and hooded cloak, confirming to Amanda that she hadn't gone home. Her hair was full of straw and face smeared with dirt. Although Miriam appeared tired, her brown eyes were alert.

Robyn ran to meet her halfway. He put a hand on her shoulder. "God's wounds, Miriam, where hast thou been? Thou hast never told me thou help—"

Miriam coolly cut him off with a scowl, and batted his hand away from her shoulder. "'Tis none of your concern!" Then she glared at Amanda. "And thou should be ashamed of thyself, acting as one of the stricken."

Amanda's face clouded over. "I-I'm sorry, Miriam, I had no other choice."

"There is always a choice, Amanda," Miriam said gruffly.

"Uh, do you think you three could catch up another time?" Jordan interrupted. "The poop squad is on the move again."

Amanda checked behind her. A few soldiers had freed themselves and were sifting through the stinky debris for their weapons.

"Come along, children," Melody said, running up. "We've got to beat the soldiers to the Rockyard Inn."

Miriam frowned. "Why art thou going thither?"

"The cellar caves will take us to the deepest cavern, where the sheriff holds their friend, John Lucas," Alan a'Dale replied.

"Yea, Much, Jean, and Tuck await us," Wil added.

"You're welcome to join us if you wish, Miriam," Melody said, starting to pick straw out of Miriam's disheveled brown hair. "We're all Robyn's friends, so the more the merrier. My name is Melody."

Amanda watched Miriam run her thumb along her bow. She checked behind her. Amanda looked too. All she saw were a couple of men in silk tights and fur-lined cloaks heading their way. One of them, a gray bearded man with a wrinkled face and vigilant eyes, pointed at them.

Miriam stiffened. "Aye, Melody, I will accompany thee, but I know a quicker way. Follow me."

Robyn grabbed Miriam's hand. "But, Miriam, where art thou—"

"Release me, Hodekin, or thou shalt be making merry with the point of my arrow!"

Robyn winced and unhanded Miriam. She nodded tersely, then waved for Melody and the rest of them to follow her. Before Amanda had time to take her next breath, Miriam raced past the pottery cart she'd stood on and jumped over a small fence.

"What was that about?" Amanda asked.

Shell-shocked, Robyn said, "'Tis most odd, the way Miriam spoke to me."

"Never mind that," Jordan said. "We'd better go or we'll lose her."

The Rockyard Inn sat against the monstrous castle rock, looking stark and out of place in the shadow of Nottingham Castle. Dark timber framed its white-washed walls, while the shaggy thatched roof resembling an unkempt sheepdog gave the inn a welcoming feel. Smoke billowed from a chimney stack, releasing the pungent, thick smell of brewing ale and roasting meat into the air. Wagons were parked in a helter-skelter manner near the inn and horses hitched to posts. Much and Jean were carrying in sacks of grain.

"Much, Jean, get thee inside!" Robyn yelled, as he ran toward them.

Much dropped the sacks and crossed his burly arms over his grimy green tunic. He stiffly shook his head. "Father will have me 'ead if I don't deliver 'is grain."

"Aye, Robyn, Much's father is not to be trifled with," Jean added.

"Yeah, well the guards looking for us will have all of our heads if they catch us," Jordan said, running past Much, and into the inn.

The moment Amanda crossed the threshold of the inn, she retched. Heavy smoke, body odor, and strong ale overwhelmed her senses. She gazed around, squinting from the smoke. The inn was almost filled to capacity. The sounds of guffawing, chortling, and cantankerous talking circled her ears the way a snake wraps around its prey. Some customers sitting at long pitted tables eyed them suspiciously, while others pointed and raised their goblets to them.

"I don't know what smells worse," Treena whispered, covering her nose. "The wagon full of poop or this inn full of patrons."

"How do people get past the stench to drink that stuff?" Ravi asked, plugging his nose.

"Betcha it's healthier than the sewage-infested water around here," Drake said.

Near one of the tables at the back, Amanda spotted three knapsacks propped against the wall. Alan a'Dale's lute and Robyn's bow and arrows had been placed on top of them. Bags of grain that Much and Jean had hauled in were slouched across the floor, looking like faceless rag dolls. Treena, Ravi, Jordan, Alan a'Dale, and Robyn headed back to gather their belongings, while Melody, Wil, and Drake walked over to where Jean was sorting out the grain.

"How may I help thee?"

Amanda whirled around. Her mouth opened, but no words escaped. A tall, bearded man with steady blue eyes and short, tidy blond hair looked down at her. He was dressed in a full length white cloak with an embroidered red cross on the left side that flared out at each end. Under his cloak, Amanda noticed he was wearing a leather vest, breeches, and worn boots. A long sword was sheathed in his belt, but she guessed it would only take him a split second to wield it if provoked.

"W-We're with Much the miller's son," Amanda blurted at the man as tall as a bear. "I was just looking for the cellar caves. Could you point me in the general direction?"

The man knitted his fair brows. "If thou wishest something from me, then 'tis my right to wish something of thee."

Amanda frowned, thinking over his offer. "You mean if I give, I get?"

Even with all the smoke in the air, the man's face lit up, as if Amanda had told him a secret she'd never shared with anyone else. He grinned down at her, his teeth as white as his cloak. "Aye, 'tis that simple, milady. Have thy friends lift a bag of grain from yon pile and follow me toward the back of my establishment."

Amanda nodded. Just as she was about to tell the others to grab a bag of grain, Miriam shrieked, "I beg of thee, let me go, Friar Tup!"

"Nay, thou must do as thy father bids, milady Miriam! Thou shalt come with me!"

The man Miriam had addressed as Friar Tup wore a long brown robe that would have brushed the floor had he been a hundred pounds lighter. The coarse rope he used as a belt strained against his girth, and the top of his head was shaved bare, leaving the rest of his hair looking like a bad bowl cut. His cheeks were roly-poly to the point of almost swallowing his thin lips. He clutched Miriam's arm and started to drag her toward the door.

Tuck growled and rushed the fat friar. Startled, he released Miriam and backed into a table full of platters of meat and pitchers of ale. Lewd laughter and cheers swallowed the air, as men started betting on who would win—the canine or the clergy. Most were pulling for Tuck.

"Friar Tup! Tuck! Friar Tup! Tuck!" Robyn shouted, as he raced over, trying to shove his bow over his shoulders.

Jean, Much, and Wil ran over to help Robyn haul Tuck away from the sniveling friar.

Miriam rubbed her arm as Amanda helped her up. "What's all that about, Miriam?"

For the first time since Amanda had met Miriam, she saw fear in her eyes. "'Tis nothing thou canst do, Amanda," she whispered.

"Come along, girls," Melody said, tossing aside her sword and reaching for their hands. "The entrance to the cellar caves is at the back of the inn."

"Aye, our quest awaits, muse," Alan a'Dale said, strumming his lute behind them.

"Rogues! Thou shall be hanged for what thou hast done!"

Amanda clasped her throat, imagining rope cutting into her skin, snapping her neck. In the doorway of the inn stood five soldiers covered in manure and hay. She winced at the stench.

The tall man in the white cloak drew his sword and blocked the soldiers from entering. "Get out of my inn, or I shall have all of thy ears to feed my swine."

Jean lunged for his staff leaning against a table and held it ready. "Aye, and a broken nose for thy trouble."

The lead soldier stiffened. "'Tis against the law to give criminals sanctuary, Sir George."

"I see only guests," Sir George said calmly, glancing around. Then he stared at Friar Tup and smirked. "Except for the friar. Thou mayest take him if thou wishes."

The soldier grunted. "Have thy way, Sir George, but thy guests must leave eventually. We will stand guard till then."

Amanda watched the stinky soldiers back out. Friar Tup ambled out as fast as his turkey legs could carry him, crossing himself at least nine times over. Sir George slammed the door, then turned and raised his sword.

"Ale on the house. 'Tis May Day after all."

The patrons cheered and whistled, clanking their tankards and goblets together and laughing like children in a candy store. Sheathing his sword, Sir George picked up a bag of barley and marched toward the back in disciplined, direct strides. As he passed Amanda he winked and said, "Thou givest, thou gettest."

With everyone's help, all the grain was piled neatly in a rectangular cave at the bottom of the stairs that led back up to the inn. Sir George suggested that they change out of their minstrel-wear and Jordan wash the blue woad off his face. Jensen didn't have to be told twice, and as for Amanda, the tunic she wore was starting to make her itch in all the wrong places.

Looking around, Amanda couldn't help but wonder about the labyrinth of caves that infiltrated the village of Nottingham. From Mortimer's hole to the dungeon to the courtyard and all throughout Nottingham, these caves seemed to be used for everything from shelters to malting rooms to businesses. Shivering at the drop in temperature, Amanda rubbed her arms briskly, trying to warm them.

"I remember my father telling me the Nottingham caves were used as bomb shelters during World War II," Melody whispered to Drake and Treena.

Treena groaned. "FYI—I think I'd feel safer above ground."

"You'd be safer in here than in an actual mine," Drake said, as he pushed his hand against the cave wall. "This sand makes for a solid base, so nothing's gonna collapse on top of us."

"It's not the collapsing part that freaks me out," Treena said, her teeth chattering. "It's what's in those dark tunnels."

Jordan snorted. "Really, Treena? You're not afraid of being squashed to death, but you're afraid of what's in the caves?"

Ravi made a scary *woo* sound. "She's afraid of what lurks beneath the surface."

"Don't worry, Treena," Amanda said. "Jockstrap's face will scare them away."

The acrid smell of rushes burning began to fill the cave as Sir George lit five torches. He passed one to Jordan, the second to Alan a'Dale, a third to Melody, and the fourth to Robyn, keeping the last torch for himself.

"Yonder are many passages stemming from this main tunnel," Sir George said. "Follow me, stay close."

Sir George led them down a series of caves all branching from underneath the Rockyard Inn. Both Sir George and Jordan lit the way with their torches. Next in line came Jean, Miriam, Melody, and Drake. They were tailed by Wil, Ravi, Alan a'Dale, Much, and Tuck, while Amanda, Treena, and Robyn brought up the rear. Along the way they passed small subterranean rooms filled with jugs and cooking pots used to make the inn's ale. A circular kiln reeked of burned barley and wheat. Amanda winced at the sharp smell.

The dampness was starting to push into Amanda's skin. Treena seemed to be dragging her feet, and they were falling behind. Amanda nudged Treena, but she didn't want to move any faster.

"Get going, Treena," Amanda said, prodding her.

Treena chewed her bottom lip. "Sorry, Amanda, but I'm not too good with things that go bump in a cave."

"Is there a problem?" Robyn asked, as he waved the torch in their faces.

"I think Treena's having a cave crisis. You know, bugs, bats, anything with antennas."

Robyn shook his head. "'Tis the truth no wiggles survive down here. Now go, before we lose them."

"What'd he say?" Treena asked.

"He said no chance of it. Nothing stays alive long enough in the caves."

Treena gulped. "N-Nothing? Does that include us?"

Shuffling down the tunnel, Amanda heard whispering going on ahead. They were almost under the castle. Another turn and they would catch up with the others. Sir George brought a finger to his lips and pointed. Amanda saw another tunnel to their left. This one seemed wider and rounder. It also appeared darker and deeper. Treena groaned again.

"'Tis where I must take my leave," Sir George said. A hint of regret lingered in his voice. "Follow yon cave. It shall take thee to where thou wishest to be."

"My first choice would be Disneyland, but finding Uncle John is a close second," Jordan said. "Thanks for helping us, Sir George."

Sir George bowed. "As a Knight Templar 'tis my duty to protect those on a pilgrimage."

"And 'tis my duty to give thee alms for thy quest, Sir George," Robyn said. He handed him the money earned from sword fighting in the street.

Sir George smiled. "I thank thee for thy patronage. I shall do my best to serve."

He started down the tunnel they had just come through and stopped. There was another passageway, barely visible, and he shone his torch against the brown wall to reveal an etched symbol. Amanda made out a triangle inverted over another triangle with a circle drawn around it.

"'Tis the Seal of Solomon," Sir George said. "Follow it. 'Twill guide thy way out, away from the inn and into Sherwood Forest. King Richard hath used this passage many a time. I wish thee safe journey, my friends."

Amanda heard *snap, crack, whoosh* as Sir George tossed his torch into the air. He was gone before it landed. She rubbed her eyes.

Treena's jaw dropped. "Now I'm officially freaked out."

"Come on, guys, let's bust Uncle John out," Jordan said as he led the way.

Tuck whined and stopped. Much grabbed his muzzle and pulled him forward.

"I don't blame you, Tuck," Treena whispered. "I don't wanna go either."

A low groan, like misery warmed over, permeated through Amanda's bones. The morose sound came from the direction they were heading. This was followed by a set of chains jingling. The hairs on the back of her neck rippled. Her shoulders tensed. She swallowed hard and as they turned a corner, braced herself for the worst.

Melody gasped. It was worse than worse. Professor Lucas was slumped across the cave floor, chained to the wall, his head down.

"Uncle John!" Jordan shouted as he started to run toward him.

As if coming to life, Professor Lucas jerked his head up. "S-Stay back, Jordan! It...it's a—"

"Trap!" a low voice cut in from the darkest part of the shadows.

Following the torches, Amanda squinted, and there, smiling like a jackal, stood Marcus Crowley. He was leaning against an arch.

She did a double take. The arch appeared similar to the Arch of Atlantis as far as stature and shape, but it had an unfathomable blackness to it, as if this was the gate to hell. Crowley snickered, sounding like a dying snake.

"Good day, Timekeepers," he said with all the sincerity of a lunatic. He stepped away from the arch and swished a hand in front of it. "I'd like to introduce you to Belial, Thirteenth Magus of the Arcane Tradition, and Master of the fifth Arch of Atlantis."

17. The Door Where Evil Dwells

Master of the fifth Arch of Atlantis? Thirteenth Magus of the Arcane Tradition? It sounded like an arrogant boast to Amanda. She glanced up toward the keystone in the arch, and her eyes widened. A black trident was set inside it. She peered into the archway and stiffened. A blob of darkness, like a shadow with no shape, filled the void. An icy, stabbing sensation, as if she were being kissed by the Grim Reaper, consumed her. She shuddered.

"Uncle John, are you okay?" Jordan asked, running over to help him up. He shone the torch over him. "Did...did Crowley hurt you?"

Professor Lucas blinked, then grunted. He reached over to tousle Jordan's hair. "I'll survive, Tiger. Just seeing you has made my day brighter."

Amanda checked over the professor. He was a little worse for wear—cuts on his face, tattered clothing, and bruised wrists from where the shackles hung. The only thing that looked untouched was his blue fishing hat. Just as Jordan let go of his uncle, Melody rushed over to inspect him. She handed Miriam the torch, then dipped into one of her pockets to retrieve the Swiss Army knife she had used to fashion Robyn's bow. Freeing a small blade, she proceeded to pick the professor's shackles. It was like watching Houdini in a skirt. The chains fell to the cave floor in a matter of seconds. Stunned, Amanda wondered where Melody had learned that trick.

Rubbing his wrists lightly, Professor Lucas winked at Melody and then turned to face Crowley. "Let them go, Marcus. They're just kids, for God's sake!"

Crowley snickered. "They're also Timekeepers, Johnny-boy, and a threat to Belial."

Melody took a step forward. "Belial's an evil parasite, Crowley! Don't you see?"

"Well now, you must be Melody Spencer," Crowley said, inclining his head. "I don't believe I've had the pleasure of a proper introduction."

"And you won't get one either, you worm-face pus-ball!" Drake spat, jumping in front of Melody.

Low, raspy laughter rolled from the arch, like it had just crawled up from hell. The black trident ominously glowed. Goose bumps rippled across Amanda's chilled skin as a voice slithered out from the arch.

"Yesss. Get mad, Drake Bailey, get mad. Don't you want to kill Crowley for leaving you for dead? I would. Yesss. I would crusssh him like a ssspider."

Drake stood still. Melody gathered Drake up in her arms and moved him farther away from the stone arch. Belial let out a rattled moan like he didn't take too kindly to Melody's motherly gesture. The trident dimmed as if it had been turned down a notch. A thought occurred to Amanda—Lilith had told them that Belial fed off of the anger, hatred, and fears of others. So when Drake got ticked, Belial got lunch. She smirked. At least she now knew not what to do. It was time for a hunger strike.

"Listen up, everyone!" Amanda said. "Don't get angry or freaked or start saying nasty things. That's what Belial feeds on."

"You mean you want us to pull a Peter Pan and think happy thoughts?" Treena asked.

"Yes, that's exactly what Amanda means," Professor Lucas said. "Positive thoughts and feelings helped me survive while I was down here. That's why Belial needs weak-minded people like Crowley to feast on, so they'll do all the dirty work for him."

Crowley laughed. "Weak-minded? I think the word you're looking for is *driven*, Johnny-boy. After all, it takes a lot of guts to go after what you want in this world."

"At what price, Crowley?" Melody asked. "Your humanity?"

Suddenly, a painful moan rose from the shadows behind where Professor Lucas had been chained. It sounded lost and pitiful.

Jordan waved his torch. "What was that?"

"Philip Marc," Crowley said smugly. "The true Sheriff of Nottingham."

Amanda squinted and made out the shape of a man leaning up against the cave wall. Her nostrils flared. The man smelled rancid, like he'd been down here a long time. His clothes appeared ripped and bloodied as if he'd faced a dragon. Melody and Miriam immediately ran to him. Melody started to undo his chains as she had done for the professor, while Miriam held the torch above her. He muttered something incoherent, then slumped to the floor. Professor Lucas and Much became human crutches to lift the tortured sheriff off the damp ground. They dragged him over to where the rest stood.

Jean fiercely banged his staff down. "Why hast thou chained Sheriff Marc?"

Crowley sneered. "He's being punished."

"Punished for what?" Amanda asked.

"For withholding information," Crowley replied, stroking his beard.

Ravi's mouth twitched. "What kind of information?"

"For not telling Belial where—"

"'Tis trickery which makes yon stone speak?" Robyn asked, interrupting Crowley. He shoved his torch inside the archway.

The black trident instantly dulled and a shriek reverberated out of the arch. Amanda flinched. She covered her ears, hoping they wouldn't bleed. *What did Robyn do to provoke the scream of the century?*

Belial moaned out a death rattle. "Crowley, you imbecile! You know I abhor light!"

Crowley drew his sword and hacked away Robyn's torch. He stomped the fire out and motioned him to get back with the others.

"God's wounds, Robyn Hodekin! Thou art such a knotty-pated simpkin!" Miriam blurted. "Anyone can see 'tis sorcery which commands yon arch."

"Robyn Hodekin?" Belial screeched. Then black laughter erupted. "Or isss he the legendary *Robin Hood* in the guissse of a boy?"

Drake groaned. "Great! Leave it to a girl to mess things up!"

"Robin Hood? Nay," Alan a'Dale said, shaking his head. Then he scratched his chin. "Though, 'twill work grand in my gest."

Amanda's stomach clenched. Belial now knew Robin Hood's true identity. The blob of blackness hissed out a laugh that sounded like nails scraping across an endless chalkboard. Jean jumped in front of them, swinging his staff as if he was preparing for a fight. Robyn pulled an arrow from his belt, placed it in his bow, and stood ready to aim. Wil drew his silver knife out of his belt and held it ready, while Tuck folded his ears back and let out a monstrous growl.

"Face it, Crowley, you're outnumbered! Let us go!" Professor Lucas demanded.

"Have you forgotten about these?" Crowley asked, swinging Drake and Treena's Babel necklaces like a pendulum. "I'd say it's time for a trade, Johnny-boy. In exchange for these two lovely necklaces, I'll take the young Robin Hood and your crystal trident. All he has to do is walk through the archway with the trident in his hands. Easy-peasy."

Drake grunted. He opened his mouth to say something, but Jordan slapped his hand over Drake's mouth. "No, Drake, don't give Belial anything to chew on."

Treena scrunched her face as if she'd been asked a tough math question. She pulled off her knapsack and started rummaging around in it, just as Professor Lucas said, "Surely you're not serious, Marcus? He's just a kid!"

"And he'll grow into the man who symbolizes hope for his people, Lucas," Crowley hissed. "I say let the people fight their own worthless battles! Now give the boy the crystal trident so that he can surrender himself to Belial. *Trust me*, it doesn't hurt a bit."

"Rogue!" Robyn yelled, as he released his arrow.

A shadowy tentacle emerged out of the arch and swiped at Robyn's arrow. Like some freaky osmosis experiment, it was absorbed instantly. The tentacle retreated as fast as it had appeared. Cold, hard laughter followed, while the black trident shone wickedly. Jean dropped his staff, and it rolled over to where Ravi stood.

Ravi reached down to grasp the staff with his artificial hand. His fingers jerked, as if he'd received an electric shock. His eyes widened.

"Are you okay?" Amanda whispered to him.

Ravi licked his lips and nodded. "Yeah. It's weird. As soon as I touched Jean's staff, a picture of a fishing rod flashed through my mind."

Amanda smiled. "Hold that thought, Ravi." She nudged Melody. "Give me that twine you used for Robyn's bow."

Melody quickly passed the roll of twine to her. There wasn't much left on it, but it was just enough.

"Here, Ravi," Amanda said. "Tie this twine to the end of Jean's pole. You're going fishing for Babels."

Then she pointed at the professor's hat, adorned with assorted fishing lures. Ravi grinned and nodded.

While Ravi was busy tying the string to the end of Jean's staff, Amanda let out a violent sneeze with enough force to turn her nostrils inside out and in the process knocked off Professor Lucas's hat with her hand. Crowley glared at her.

"*Gesundheit*," Professor Lucas whispered.

Amanda sniffed, wiping her nose. "Stupid allergies."

She glanced over her shoulder and frowned. The blue hat landed too far behind them to pluck off a lure. Flustered, Amanda rubbed her face. Ravi's prosthesis began to pulsate, as if it were coming to life. It twitched, back and forth, back and forth, back and forth, until his hand jumped off his stump—just as it had done when he had tried to stop Jordan. It landed on the ground and started to scuttle toward the professor's hat. Amanda and Ravi watched in awe, as the fingers acted like spider's legs while it scurried across the cave floor. When Ravi's hand reached the hat, it burrowed underneath it and scampered back to him as if it were an obedient dog returning to its master.

"I think I could really get to like this, Amanda," Ravi whispered, a smile filling his face.

Ravi picked up the hat, popped his prosthesis back on, and pulled off a lure before anyone else saw what had happened. A golden lure with six barbed hooks attached to its underbelly was Ravi's choice. Amanda smirked. It was perfect for bottom feeders like Crowley. While hidden behind her, Ravi secured the lure to the end of the twine, gave it a good tug, and let it drop.

"Ready?" she asked quietly.

"Ready for the catch of the day," he whispered.

Suddenly, a light danced across their eyes. Treena held out her illuminated cell phone she'd retrieved from her knapsack. "Need a light? There's an app for that," she whispered.

Amanda had seen Belial's allergic reaction to Robyn's torch. Treena's lit phone would be just the diversion to keep that hissing blob of hate from interfering with Ravi's cast. She nodded. "Be a star and shine, Treena."

"When I cast out this line—"

"I know," Treena cut in. "Throw a little light Belial's way."

Crowley snickered. "Well, John, time's running out, and Belial loathes to be kept waiting. Decide now, or I'll throw these Babels to Belial!"

Before Professor Lucas could answer, Ravi let the lure fly. It was a perfect cast, considering he didn't have a lightweight rod and proper reel. The line wound tightly around Crowley's hand, and Ravi yanked back hard as if he'd landed the biggest fish of his life.

"Arggah!" Crowley yelled.

As if on cue, Treena pitched her glowing cell phone into the mouth of the arch. "Hey, Belial, time for your wake-up call!"

The black trident went lifeless just as a bone-shattering howl exploded through the archway. Crowley dropped his sword and released the Babel necklaces as the lure's barbed hooks dug into his skin. He fell to his knees with a scream of pain, almost rivaling Belial. Amanda lunged to scoop up the necklaces and tossed them to Ravi, who distributed the Babels to their rightful owners. It was teamwork at its best.

"Y-You'll regret this, boy!" Crowley shrieked, glaring at Ravi.

"The only thing I regret is not having a bigger hook, fish-lips." Ravi smirked as he flipped the professor his hat.

"Okay, everybody, let's move!" Professor Lucas yelled. He fumbled for the hat and plopped it on his head.

"Right behind you, Uncle!" Jordan shouted. He looked over his shoulder. "Do your thing, Wil! Cut the sucker loose!"

Wil reached out with his knife and cut the twine imprisoning Crowley. This action launched Crowley backward into the stone archway. Like a scene out of a horror movie, Crowley was sucked into the swirling dark blob. A grotesque gurgle came out of Belial, like Crowley had left a bad after taste. Something was burped out of the arch. It slid across the cave floor and landed by Treena's feet. It was her cell phone, melted and mangled and fizzling.

Treena winced. "Guess I should have gone with a better long distance plan."

"Zounds, Ravi, thou art the best fisherman my eyes hath seen!" Jean shouted.

"Thanks, Jean, but I think I'll stick to a lighter rod!" Ravi replied, tossing Jean his staff.

Miriam and Treena led the way out of the cave, while Tuck became their shadow. They were followed by Much and Professor Lucas dragging the unconscious Sheriff Marc. Next went Jean, Jordan, Drake, Wil, and Robyn. Only Alan a'Dale, Amanda, Ravi, and Melody remained. The sound of rattling chains halted their exodus and made them look back at the arch. The black trident turned a ghostly gray hue and out popped a man, as if Belial had birthed him. The man got up cautiously and started to smooth his attire out. He was dressed like he had stepped out of another time zone.

Melody gasped. "W-Who are you?"

The man looked at them sideways. "Maxwell J. Tarbush," he croaked, as if he hadn't used his voice in a very long time.

Tarbush raised his right arm and pulled down his sleeve to reveal nothing but a burned fleshy stump. A line of black slime dripped from the corner of Tarbush's mouth, and he sneered as he wiped it away.

"'Tis time we take our leave, muse," Alan a'Dale said, grabbing Amanda's hand and leading her toward the tunnel where the others had disappeared.

"W-What do you want, Tarbush?" Ravi asked nervously, while Melody tugged on his arm to follow.

Maxwell J. Tarbush grinned wickedly. "I want another chance at lady luck," he replied. "This time I'm determined to come up aces."

18. Even the Score

manda's adrenaline was pumping as she followed Alan a'Dale through the cave's opening. In a way, she felt like Alice leaving the Mad Hatter and the grinning Cheshire cat behind. *Good riddance,* she thought. She whirled around and waited for the rest to emerge from Wonderland. Thirty seconds flew by and still no Ravi, no Melody and no white rabbit made an appearance. Her stomach churned as if a butter knife was scraping out her guts.

"'Tis odd," Alan a'Dale said, snuffing his torch. "Thy friends were behind us."

Breathing hard, Amanda nodded. This was getting spooky. "M-M-Maybe…Tarbush caught up with them."

"Tarbush! He's alive?" Jordan asked.

"I-I wouldn't exactly call it alive," Amanda replied, holding her chest. "H-He's more like Belial's zombie-puppet."

"Come, Tuck!" Robyn said, slapping his thigh. "We shall go back after them."

"No, Robyn, wait!" Professor Lucas shouted as he and Much propped Sheriff Marc up against an old oak tree.

Jean stepped in front of Robyn. "Nay, Robyn, Belial wants thee!"

"Aye, coz, 'tis not wise," Wil added.

Much ambled up and slapped Robyn across the back of the head. "And thou callest me a simpkin? 'Twould be mad to go back in yon cave!"

Robyn rubbed his head, smacked Much back, and then pushed Jean. "Leave off, Jean!"

"Robyn, wait!" Amanda grabbed his arm. "You've got an archery tournament to win. Remember what I told you—about the chicks?" She winked at him.

A silly smile erupted across Robyn's face. He stole a look at Miriam and blushed.

Ravi barreled out of the cave, followed closely by Melody. They slammed into Jean, who banged into Robyn, sending him flying through the air to land on Sheriff Marc's lap.

Amanda's whole body sighed. "Where were you guys?"

"I-I-I tripped," Melody stammered. "R-Ravi helped...me up."

"Robyn! Robyn Hodekin...art thou hurt?" Miriam cried, as she raced after him.

The sheriff's head twitched back and forth, and he started to mumble. At first, he was hard to understand. Then his words got clearer. "R-Robin? Robin Hood? Thief! Villain! Poacher! I will hunt thee down till the day I die, Robin Hood!"

Miriam stopped dead in her tracks. Startled, Robyn scrambled away from Sheriff Marc.

"Sheriff Marc hath never said such hateful things of Robyn before," Miriam said.

"What did Belial do to him down there, Prof?" Drake asked.

"Poisoned his mind, I guess," Professor Lucas replied, helping Melody up. "Being down there for as long as he was, in the company of a dark, evil mind, would make anyone go mad."

"I-I agree, John," Melody replied, trying to grasp her breath. "Tarbush serves Belial now, and I believe he has taken over from where Crowley left off."

Drake frowned. "What happened to Crowley?"

"That douche-bag was sucked back into the archway and got what he deserved," Ravi replied, crawling out of a bush. He pulled out a small forked branch stuck in his pants and flung it aside. "We gotta get outta here before Tarbush catches us."

"Nay, we shall stand and fight the rogue!" Wil spat.

"No," Treena blurted, pumping her fist in the air. "We need to get Robyn to the tournament. He has to follow his destiny! He has to rob from the rich to give to the poor!"

Wil stared at Treena intensely. "Now thou speakest the truth to me!"

Amanda groaned. "I don't think that's what Lilith had in mind when she recruited us to be Timekeepers, Treena."

"Then let me show you what Belial has in mind for you and the rest of your time-meddling friends, girl!" a harsh voice hissed from behind Amanda.

Amanda twisted around. There, standing at the mouth of the cave was Max Tarbush. Being out in the daylight didn't do him any justice. A thin man with ghostly white hair, bushy sideburns, and a moustache that screamed "shave me," he wore a dark long overcoat that flared at the waist and black stove-pipe pants. His complexion was pallid, washed over, like that of a creepy mortician. A faded, jagged incision ran across his forehead as if he'd been mistaken for a Thanksgiving turkey.

Tuck gave him a warning growl, but all he did was laugh.

Professor Lucas rushed over and stood in front of Amanda and the other kids. He crossed his arms defiantly and glared at him. "I suggest that you crawl back to wherever you came from, Tarbush! You're unarmed and outnumbered!"

Tarbush laughed again. A bubble of black ooze blew out of one nostril. He snorted it away like an unwanted booger. "Unarmed? I suggest that you take a closer look."

Tarbush pulled out two playing cards from his coat pocket. They looked ordinary, harmless in fact, but when he simultaneously dealt the pair of cards through the air, they became lethal weapons. One card whizzed toward Melody's head like one of Jordan's fastballs. Jean put his staff out in time and intercepted it. The other card whined in Miriam's direction. Robyn was there, holding out his bow across her body as Tarbush's card sliced into it. His bow split, cracked, and half fell to the ground with the queen of spades stuck in it.

Miriam gasped. "Oh, Robyn! Thy bow. 'Tis ruined."

The five of spades hummed as it protruded from Jean's staff. The professor reached over to pull it out, then winced and checked his hand. One of his fingers was bleeding. Amanda guessed the card was made of a lightweight metal—like a razor blade, but sharper.

"Oh yes, and as for being outnumbered," Tarbush said. He flicked his tongue out like a snake and whistled hard.

Soldiers who must have been patrolling the forest yelled out, "'Tis this way!"

Tarbush pulled out another card. He held it ready. His reptilian lip quivered. "I'll take Hood and the crystal trident now!"

Treena moaned. "Where's a secret weapon when you need one?"

Amanda stiffened. Her body tingled, as if sending her a secret text. She blinked. "I believe I can help us with that, Treena."

Swiftly, Amanda scooped up the forked branch Ravi had discarded and jumped behind Jordan. She unzipped his backpack and started to rifle through it.

"What are you doing?" Jordan whispered from the corner of his mouth.

"Just stand still and block Tarbush's view," she answered. "Where is it? Where is it?"

"Where is what?" Treena asked.

She didn't answer Treena. She'd found it. Gritting her teeth, Amanda pulled it out with one snap of her wrist, cup and all. Treena's eyes bugged.

"You were looking for Jordan's jockstrap? You're sick, Amanda," Treena muttered.

"You see a jockstrap. I see a weapon," Amanda explained, wiggling the forked branch in front of Treena. "Haven't you ever fired a slingshot before?"

Treena smirked. She looked down and found a round rock by her foot. She plucked it up and passed it to Amanda. "Make it count, Huckleberry."

Amanda nodded and quickly assembled the makeshift slingshot. She could hear heavy footsteps advancing toward them. Branches cracked, the earth shook, and small animals scurried away. She wiped the beading sweat from her brow. The soldiers were getting closer, the Sheriff of Nottingham was waking up, and Max Tarbush stood waiting, black slime trickling from his mouth. Amanda counted to three in her head, then stepped out from behind Jordan, pulled back the strap, and released the rock.

Smack! Amanda's shot hit Tarbush square on the chin and sent him screeching backward toward the cave's entrance.

Miriam cheered. "Thou goest, girl!"

"Eww, look!" Treena squealed, pointing at Tarbush.

The razor card Tarbush was holding had sliced into his left cheek above his moustache. He shrieked, floundered, and kicked on the ground in front of the cave as black slime spurted from the deep gash—blinding, torturing, and imprisoning him. Amanda grimaced.

"Looks like Tarbush had to fold his hand," Ravi said, grinning.

Jordan laughed. "Yeah, apparently Amanda doesn't like to bluff."

"Come on guys, let's make like a tree and leaf!" Drake yelled.

"What about the Sheriff of Nottingham?" Treena asked.

Professor Lucas shook his head sternly. "We'll have to leave him, Treena. He'll be fine, his men will find him. As far as history is concerned, it has remained unchanged—the Sheriff of Nottingham is *now* Robin Hood's sworn enemy."

"Yes, John, but only we know the *truth* behind it," Melody said before they all disappeared into the shelter of the dark forest.

An hour later, with a few of Robyn Hodekin's shortcuts, found them in the heart of the May Day festivities. The tournament had already started. Not surprisingly, Sir Guy of Gisborne led the score. However, there was one big problem keeping Robyn from entering the tournament—the sheriff's men were posted everywhere. Hidden behind one of the vendors' carts, Amanda and Miriam spotted the Sheriff of Nottingham, dressed in a fresher cloak and cleaner hose, standing next to Max Tarbush. Amanda squinted. A deeply-etched black scar ran down the side of Tarbush's face now, making him appear paler and meaner. She grunted. Somehow, Belial knew that they were going to be here and seemed to be covering all his bases.

"'Tis most odd," Miriam blurted.

Startled, Amanda glanced toward Miriam. "What?"

"I have searched the grounds over and over, yet cannot find him."

"Who?"

Miriam sighed. "Robert, the Earl of Huntingdon," she replied. "I met him two summers past with my father at an archery tourney. He is ten years my senior and was smitten with me."

Amanda caught the tone of sadness in Miriam's voice. "How smitten?" she asked.

"Smitten enough to ask Father for my hand in marriage," Miriam whispered. "Father accepted the earl's most recent proposal. The high tax the sheriff places upon our manor is too much. Huntingdon offers a handsome sum for me, enough to run the household for a goodly while."

"That's the reason you never went home last night, isn't it?" Amanda pressed. "And those men you spotted in Nottingham, they were out looking for you, weren't they?"

"Aye," Miriam replied quietly, as if the pluck had fizzled out of her.

Amanda needed to know more. "Do you like this earl guy?"

Miriam's face puckered as if getting ready to puke. "Nay, 'tis the truth the earl looks like a pock-marked eel with greasy, black hair. And his manners...well thou will understand when I tell thee Much possesses more!"

Amanda's jaw dropped. "Does...Robyn know?"

"Nay," Miriam replied, shaking her head. "It appears he has found someone else."

"Who?"

Miriam looked Amanda in the eye. "Thee."

Amanda coughed. "Me? What would make you think that?"

"I saw thee and Robyn together in the meadow this morning. I saw him kiss thy hand."

Amanda's eyes widened. It had been Miriam she saw running through the forest. Amanda shook her head vehemently. "But, Miriam, Robyn was just thanking me for helping him see things clearly. You've gotta believe me, all the archery lessons and winning the tournament is for *you*, not me!"

Miriam gasped. Her face reddened. "Me?"

Amanda grinned. "Thee."

Then Amanda's body prickled all over. *Pock-marked eel. Greasy, black hair.* She smirked, nudged her newfound friend and said, "Hey, Miriam, maybe the Earl of Huntingdon will show up for the tournament after all! Let's get back to the others. I've got an idea."

It would be a quick makeover at best, but Amanda had faith in Ravi's skills. If he could transform himself and White Pines' Golden Jock into repulsive lepers, then he could surely change Robyn Hodekin into the equally revolting Earl of Huntingdon. Much and Wil were sent out to round up the necessary clothing fit for this particular, pompous earl—an oversized silk tunic with matching breeches and a fur-lined embroidered cloak. Professor Lucas swiftly constructed a pair of wooden stilts from branches, as Miriam had advised that the earl stood as tall as the professor. Luckily, Ravi had enough liquid latex and wax left to pockmark Robyn's face, while Treena offered her services and applied her tube of hair tint to darken his hair. All in all, when the transformation process was complete, Robyn emerged from the cocoon of Ravi Sharma's cleverness into the full-fledged, butt-ugly Earl of Huntingdon. Amanda was impressed. So was everyone else.

"Zounds!" Jean said. "Even I would not recognize thee, Robyn."

Alan a'Dale flinched. "God's teeth, thou art as comely as a hog!"

Tuck growled his displeasure.

Robyn tried to grin, but the waxy face craters wouldn't allow him. So he nodded and said, "I only hope to fool Sheriff Marc."

"Thou willst, Robyn," Miriam said. "Just remember, the earl tends to cough a lot and then spits it all out." She puckered her face in disgust.

Treena gagged. "Just when you thought you'd heard it all."

"Is he ready?" Melody asked. "They've almost gone through all of the archers."

Robyn turned on his stilts—the silky breeches concealing them perfectly—and bowed regally toward Melody. She smiled and curtsied.

"Hey, what about Robyn's bow?" Jordan asked. "It got sliced in half."

Miriam sighed. "Here, Hodekin." She passed Robyn her longbow and arrows. "'Twill do thee well on the archery field."

Robyn attempted to smile, but it was pointless. "I thank thee, Miriam. I shall take good care of thy bow." He slid a finger over its length.

Miriam shrugged. "'Tis thine to keep."

Robyn glanced at her warily. "But, Miriam, thou lovest thy bow."

Miriam glanced Amanda's way. She shook her head. "'Tis time I grew up, Hodekin."

"You'd best get going, Robyn," Melody said, patting his shoulder. "And remember what I taught you—above all, focus first."

"Aye, milady," Robyn replied. "'Tis the whole task of being an archer, not just hitting the target, which makes thee great."

"You taught him that?" Professor Lucas asked in astonishment. Then he winked at her. "Ever thought of becoming a professor?"

Melody giggled. "And give up my job as a Timekeeper? Never!"

Amanda watched Robyn hobble off into the crowd to get to the end of the line of archery contestants. Miriam had explained that the tournament included three different tests of skill in order to eliminate the worst from the best. The first was distance shooting— a test of endurance, where the archers must shoot two rounds of six arrows on a target fifty strides away, then four rounds of six arrows on a target seventy-five strides away, and finally six rounds of six arrows on a target one hundred strides away. The second test was speed shooting where the archer must shoot as many arrows as possible into a target. Miriam said that the best count she had ever seen was eighteen arrows. The final test, which sounded like the most exciting to Amanda, was the elimination round. Only one arrow was used, and the archer who came closest to hitting the bull's-eye won the tournament and the prize—a silver arrow and purse full of gold.

Keeping low, Amanda, her fellow Timekeepers, and Robyn's friends hid behind a tent surrounded by red and white banners. Alan a'Dale sat cross-legged next to her, plucking on his lute. He'd mumble out a few words, shake his head, growl and grunt, then start again.

Amanda watched with anticipation as Robyn showed his true skill with the longbow throughout the first event. Every now and then, she heard Robyn cough then spit on the ground. Even the crowd seemed pleased and cheered him on. Robyn was definitely the underdog in this tournament. Sir Guy still led the way, but Robyn was catching up with each arrow he nocked. The second event proved Robyn definitely had the right stuff, as he shot an amazing twenty-two arrows to Sir Guy's nineteen. The tournament was now tied.

They were finally down to the last event when Amanda noticed that all of Robyn's arrows were either broken or split. He would need replacements and soon. Slowly, Amanda crept away and started searching the grounds, careful not to be spotted by the sheriff's men. She spied a pile of arrows next to the entrance of another tent. She smiled. This was Robyn's lucky day. Amanda crouched behind carts and people and lurked in the shadows until she reached the tent. She scored a fistful of arrows, then turned to head back, but was stopped short by an armored hand on her shoulder. Swallowing hard, she followed the gleaming arm up to stare at the biggest, most intimidating knight she'd ever seen glaring down at her. His gauntlets were spiked and his helm had feathers sprouting out of its top like a hiccupping peacock. A somber growl erupted through his visor. Amanda closed her eyes, feeling the knight's steely hand start to squeeze her shoulder, and hoped he wouldn't pop off her head like a ripened zit.

Clank! Amanda opened her eyes, thinking someone had hit an iron wall. The knight eased up on her shoulder, dropped his arm, wobbled, then started to plunge toward her. She sidestepped her metallic nemesis in time. The knight landed face first into a mud puddle. Professor Lucas stood in front of her, swinging a club with metal spikes. He didn't seem very pleased with her.

"And just what do you think you're doing, young lady?" the professor asked.

She grinned like a sharp sales lady. He didn't seem to buy it though, so Amanda cleared her throat and said, "Robyn needs more arrows, Professor. All of his are busted."

Professor Lucas rubbed his stubbly chin and nodded. "Then we'd better get him some. Quick, help me drag this knight into that tent. I'll put on his armor to hide my identity from Tarbush and the sheriff so that I can deliver the arrows to Robyn."

Amanda rallied the others and brought them back to the tent. Inside, Jean and Miriam helped Professor Lucas on with the armor—which took a lot of grunting and groaning on the professor's behalf. Some of the armor fit, some of it didn't. Melody found a quiver, and Treena looked for the straightest and sharpest arrows to put in it. Jean strapped the sword, scabbard and belt around the professor's waist while Miriam hastily placed the helm on his head. There—one knight in shining armor ready for duty.

A gasp was uttered near the tent's entrance. "What hast thou done with milord, rogues!"

Amanda turned. A boy with tangled blond hair and killer blue eyes glared at them. He tried to scowl, but he was too pretty. The dark, flowing tunic and breeches he wore made him look almost harmless, with the exception of a long knife strapped to his belt. He reached for the knife about the same time Jordan whacked him from behind with a shield. His eyes rolled, and down he went with a thud. Tuck wandered over to sniff him, then lifted his leg and peed on him.

"Who's the douche?" Drake asked.

"'Tis the knight's squire," Jean replied, poking him with his staff.

"Aye, and a soggy one at that, I'd wager," Much added.

Miriam groaned. "God's wounds, he will be missed on the field. 'Tis the truth, a squire's duty is to follow and serve his knight."

Amanda looked at the grounded squire, then glanced up at Jordan. She smirked. "Then the knight shall have his squire. How about it, Jockstrap? The squire looks like he'd be about your size. All you'd have to do is carry the arrows and keep your face covered."

Melody snapped her fingers. "That's brilliant, Amanda! This way, everything will appear normal and their moves won't be suspicious."

Jordan's mouth twitched. "Not brilliant. Not gonna do it. Not wearing something that Tuck did his business on."

"Oh, come on, Jordan," Treena said. "There's a hooded cloak and fresh pair of hose on the table. Just wear them over your clothes. What have you got to lose?"

Jordan frowned. "My dignity. I don't do hose."

Drake and Ravi stifled a laugh. Melody waved them off.

"We all have to make sacrifices, Jordan," Professor Lucas said, pushing up his visor. "What do you say, Tiger? We'd be a team."

Jordan grunted. "Easy for you to say. You get to wear the cool armor." He sighed deeply. Amanda could tell Jordan was caving fast. "Fine, I'll do it, but if anyone says one thing about this when we get back home, I swear I'll—"

"Lighten up, Jockstrap, your secret's safe with us," Amanda cut in. "Besides, we're Timekeepers, who we gonna tell?"

After a quick change and some primping and preening, Jordan was good to go. Drake offered to carry his backpack while he escorted his uncle down to the field to offer Robyn the arrows as a gift. From inside the knight's tent, Amanda watched the professor clank down the hill, followed by Jordan, trying desperately not to pull up his baggy hose. Both Drake and Ravi were still trying not to laugh. As Professor Lucas and Jordan got closer to Robyn, the crowd went wild.

A spectator yelled out, "Yea, 'tis Sir Gavin the Just!"

"Who?" Treena asked.

Much snorted loudly. He slapped his forehead.

"What's up with him?" Drake asked.

Miriam shook her head. "'Tis not good. The people think they cheer their champion, Sir Gavin, a goodly knight who wins many tourneys. The crowd will demand a tilt."

"What's a tilt?" Ravi asked.

"They will wish to see a show of strength and prowess," Jean explained.

"Meaning?" Treena asked.

Melody slapped her forehead. "Bloody hell, they want to see John joust."

Amanda chewed her bottom lip. She did not want to see two knights on their armored horses charging at each other with long, pointy lances. Amanda wanted to see Robyn win the archery contest so that she and her time traveling cohorts could go home to White Pines.

"Do you think the prof knows anything about jousting?" Drake asked.

Ravi grunted. "Probably about as much as Jordan knows about wearing hose."

There was a sudden hush in the crowd as Sheriff Marc sauntered over to stand next to Professor Lucas. He waved his arms in the air.

"Good people of Nottingham, thou shall have thy day! After my coz, Sir Guy, defeats the *lucky* Earl of Huntingdon with his next shot, Sir Gavin has agreed to delight you with his skills on the jousting field!"

Cheers, claps, and shouts ripped through the air.

A nasty jolt expressed through Sir Gavin's armor told Amanda that Professor Lucas had agreed to no such thing. It was all a political ploy—the sheriff's way of manipulating the people of

Nottingham into thinking he cared about their wants and needs. Sheriff Marc led the professor off of the field so that the final shots could be taken. Jordan, with his head covered and down, shuffled over to where Robyn stood and passed him the quiver of arrows. Good. At least Robyn got what he needed. Jordan stalled momentarily and Amanda swore that she saw him flip Robyn a thumbs up sign.

Sir Guy, who was dressed completely in black, nocked his arrow, studied the target for a moment, then pulled back on his string and let the arrow loose. It was a perfect shot. Bull's-eye. Dead center. Amanda gulped.

Next up was the Earl of Huntingdon—alias Robyn Hodekin, a.k.a. Robin Hood. He bowed before the cheering people and took his stance. Robyn carefully chose an arrow from his quiver and raised his bow. He calmly nocked his arrow, pulled it back, then paused for a least a minute, as if he were in a deep trance.

"Hurry up, Huntingdon!" Sir Guy heckled. "I would like to go spend my prize money before the tavern closes!"

Robyn ignored his jeers. He seemed to be in another world. Amanda knew this world well. It was the same place she visited when composing a poem. She smiled dreamily just as Robyn let his arrow go. It flew straight into Sir Guy's arrow and split it in two. Amanda's eyes bulged at the moment of impact. Robyn had bettered his best! The crowd went crazy, clapping, stomping, and laughing as Sir Guy fell to his knees and buried his face in his hands.

The sheriff didn't look too pleased as he marched over to Robyn and awarded him his prize. Robyn hungrily grabbed the purse of gold, stuffed it down his breeches, and then held up the silver arrow to share with the people of Nottingham. He started to back away but didn't get far because a rut in the grass twisted his foot around. Stumbling, Robyn went down, fast and hard. He dropped the silver arrow as his stilts were ripped away from his body.

Sheriff Marc glared at him. "What trickery is this?" Then he gasped. "Robin Hood! Guards, seize yon rogue!"

Two guards roughly plucked Robyn up. Tarbush stormed over, grabbed Robyn's face, and viciously squeezed it. Wax craters popped off and dropped to the ground. He laughed wickedly, making the hairs on Amanda's arms rise. She shuddered as Tarbush dove into his jacket pocket and pulled out a set of playing cards.

They glittered in the sunlight, and Amanda knew they were the same metallic razor cards he'd used to attack them earlier.

"We gotta do something," Drake said.

"But what? We can't fight a whole army of the sheriff's men," Ravi replied. "That would be suicide!"

Panicking, Amanda reached for the Timekeepers' log to look for some kind of clue they could use to help Robyn. She stared at the riddle she had written what seemed a lifetime ago. She read it over again and again. Nothing clicked for her. The sound of a lute strumming near the tent broke her concentration.

"Muse? Where art thou?" Alan a'Dale asked as his feet padded through the grass.

She rolled her eyes. "In here, Alan."

Alan a'Dale swaggered into the tent like a rooster claiming his hen. "I'm done with my gest, muse. Listen to my first verse."

Amanda shook her head. "Alan, I don't have time—" His music drowned out the crowd momentarily, forcing her to pay attention to his lyrics, to hear what he had to say.

"Robin Hood in Sherwood stood. Hooded and hosed and shod. Four and twenty arrows he shot. And no one thought he could." Alan a'Dale sang, whistled, and plucked. "And no one thought he could—"

Her body hummed in harmony listening to Alan's music. The answer to the Timekeeper riddle hit her like a bolt from the blue. Yes, Ravi was right—they couldn't fight a whole army—at least not with weapons. But they could fight with *words*. Words of power and justice that would restore the balance Belial had disrupted here.

Amanda banged the log shut. "Even the score! We've gotta even the score!"

"Great. Amanda's popped a few brain cells," Drake muttered.

"No, listen, Drake, remember what you said to Crowley? About how Timekeepers are here to create chaos so that order can continue?"

Drake nodded. "So?"

"So it's time to do just that! We have to start spreading the *good news* about the *real* Robin Hood. Tell as many people as we can what we've learned about him, about his adventures, and what he does for the poor of Nottingham. That way, the people will side with Robyn. It's not lies, it's the truth. We have to split up and tell everybody we can find about this living legend!"

Alan a'Dale stopped playing. "Dost thou wish me to share my gest with the people, muse?"

Amanda laughed and hugged him. "Yes. Share it with as many people as you can, Alan. Make your gest your quest."

Alan a'Dale hugged Amanda fiercely back. "I shall wander the countryside far and wide, and share my gest with other minstrels. 'Tis my promise to thee, muse." Then he let her go, bowed, and before leaving the tent, the wandering jongleur turned and winked. "I bid thee farewell, Amanda."

Melody snapped her fingers. "Yes, it all makes sense now. Belial changed things by turning Sheriff Marc against Robyn, so we must even the score—balance what has been done by delivering the truth to the people. Come on, everyone, we don't have much time! We'll meet back on this hill when everyone's done!"

Treena groaned. "Too bad we couldn't just Tweet the good stuff about Robyn."

Much scrunched his pudgy face. "Why would thou want us to tweet like birds?"

"Never mind!" Amanda, Ravi, Drake, and Melody yelled together as they exited the tent.

The Timekeepers hit the streets of Nottingham, spreading the good deeds of Robyn Hodekin. They were talking so fast that some people were getting Robyn's name mixed up, while others got the message right away. Robin Hood? Robert Fitzooth? Robert, Earl of Huntingdon? The worst for taking information were the monks. They kept asking about Tuck's origins—and got it all wrong when someone yelled fire. Somehow Tuck became a friar. It got more confusing as Amanda tried to explain things. People started gossiping that Robyn lived in Sherwood Forest instead of Robert Fitzooth's manor, and "Little" Jean suddenly became John because someone had pronounced Jean's name with a mouthful of bread and cheese. It spread like wildfire.

When Amanda had told as many people as she could find about Robyn, his friends, and their good deeds, she hustled back up the hill. She reached the top gasping and gulping fresh air. Amanda hooded her eyes with a hand and waited for Belial's neatly lined dominoes to start falling over.

Suddenly, mob mentality kicked in, and the people got enraged. They demanded Robyn's release. Crowds began shoving the guards, chanting angry threats and throwing rotten vegetables at them. Max

Tarbush clutched the front of Robyn's tunic and dragged him away from the encroaching horde. He chortled again, then fanned out his deck of metallic cards and stuck them under the base of Robyn's throat. Amanda clasped her neck. She knew Tarbush was capable of anything, even if it meant killing Robyn to give Belial the outcome his evil heart desired—no Robin Hood, no symbol of hope, no history of a legendary hero. Gone, erased, deleted with the flick of madman's wrist.

Then Amanda caught sight of Jordan winding through the crowd. Something was in his hands. He held it in a familiar way, as if it were a football. Jordan's hood was pulled back, his left hand methodically slapping against whatever he was clutching. He appeared to be pacing, looking for an opening. Amanda removed her hand from her throat and continued to stare at Jordan's odd behavior. Whatever he was doing, he seemed focused on his intention. Jordan suddenly stood still, nodded, then hurled what Amanda realized was a deformed turnip toward the back of Max Tarbush's head. It whacked him hard and threw him off balance. The impact caused Tarbush to release his razor cards, giving Robyn enough time to weasel out of his hold. He lunged for his prize—the silver arrow—and plunged it into Tarbush's stomach before he had time to regain his weapons or his wits.

An enraged screech escaped Tarbush's mouth. Amanda covered her mouth. Black slime oozed out of his eyes, mouth, nostrils, and stomach, saturating his entire body at an incredible rate. His body gurgled, bubbled, and fizzled as if his insides were boiling over, reaching the point of no return. What was left of Maxwell J. Tarbush stumbled backward, tripped into a pile of manure, and dissolved in it, leaving Robyn's silver arrow behind, untarnished.

Jordan sprinted over, plucked the arrow out of the manure, and handed it to Robyn. He yelled something about team spirit and chest bumped Robyn. Grinning, Robyn clasped Jordan around the shoulders and slapped him roughly. Amanda shook her head. *Boys will be boys.*

Hearing harsh breathing coming from each side of her, Amanda turned to find Miriam, Treena, Drake, Ravi, and Much returning from their heralding. She hooded her eyes with a hand. Melody, Jean, and Wil were at the bottom of the hill, still talking to some of the townspeople.

"OMG!" Treena yelled, still huffing. She pointed. "T-The sheriff and his men...they're heading for Robyn and Jordan!"

Startled, Amanda cast her eyes back in time to witness the sheriff, with his sword drawn, running toward Robyn and Jordan. He had managed to thwart the ranting crowd and seemed hell-bent on finishing what Belial had started. However, Sheriff Marc didn't see the white horse approaching fast on his right flank. Amanda smiled. Sir Gavin the Just—a.k.a. Professor Lucas —maneuvered his steed over enough to cut the sheriff off and knock him down, then galloped over to where Jordan and Robyn waited. He hoisted the boys up on the horse just as Sheriff Marc got back on his feet. The muddied sheriff bellowed a curse, wielded his sword, and started to charge again.

"Robyn Hodekin!" Miriam screamed out. "Thou art my *champion!*"

Robyn looked directly at Miriam. Even Amanda could feel the intensity of their connection. He nodded, pulled his bow from his shoulders, nocked the silver arrow, aimed it at the advancing sheriff, and let it go. The sheriff's sword was shot out of his hand, causing him to stumble and fall. His men scattered as the cheering crowd rushed toward Sheriff Marc, pelting him with rotten vegetables and fresh cow dung.

Amanda's jaw dropped when she spotted a familiar face leading the pack. "Mortimer!" she shouted.

Mortimer stopped and glanced up the hill. Amanda waved at him. A bright yellow tunic and green pants had replaced his tattered clothing, and his white hair was clean and cut. He placed a hand over his brow and squinted momentarily.

"Amanda? 'Tis thee?"

Amanda cupped her mouth with her hands. "Yes! Good to see you're free, Mortimer!"

"Aye! Thou hast brought me and my people luck! Bless thee, Amanda!" Then Mortimer turned and resumed his assault on the wayward sheriff.

Amanda clapped and whistled as Sir Gavin saluted the people of Nottingham. The crowd opened up a pathway for their knight, his squire, and their newfound champion to let them pass while poor Sheriff Marc was getting pummeled. The horse kicked the ground, reared, and galloped toward the hill where Amanda and the others were observing.

Robyn jumped down first, followed by Jordan, who quickly peeled off his squire hose and cloak and chucked them. Professor Lucas dismounted slowly, groaning in discomfort. Melody, Jean, and Wil reached the crest of the hill to finally join them, out of breath and clapping. The professor pulled off his feathered helm and took a deep breath. His cheeks were ruddy, his hair was damp, and sweat dripped down the sides of his face.

He shook his head. "Whew! I don't think I'm cut out for knighthood."

Melody smiled and walked up to him. With the sleeve of her blouse she gently blotted his sweaty face. "I don't know about that, John. I'd say you're skills on the jousting field definitely delighted me."

The professor's face turned beet red.

Drake ran up and high-fived Jordan. "That was wicked-awesome, Jordan. You nailed Tarbush good! That had to be your best throw this year!" Drake slid Jordan's knapsack off his shoulder and handed it over to him.

Jean slapped Robyn on the back. "Well done, Robyn! Thou art a longbow man after all!"

"Aye, coz, 'tis the truth," Wil added with a grin. "Even the young maidens from the village talk about thee!"

Miriam made a noise that sounded like a pig's snort.

Robyn went into his breeches, pulled out the leather purse full of the gold he'd been awarded, and tossed it to Miriam. He sheepishly smiled. "I won for thee, Miriam. 'Twill be enough to carry thy household a goodly year or more."

Miriam stared at the pouch. Her thumb stroked the soft leather. "But...art thou not staying with us?" she asked. There was a hint of sadness in her voice.

Robyn shook his head. "Nay, Miriam, 'tis too dangerous for thee and thy father. Sheriff Marc will try to hunt me down."

"Zounds, then we shall form a band and live in the protection of Sherwood Forest," Jean announced as he banged the ground with his staff.

"Aye, Robyn," Wil said. "We will become the foxes whilst the sheriff and his men become the chickens."

"Aye and thou knowest how me and Tuck love to eat chickens," Much added, as he patted his big belly and stroked Tuck's shaggy head.

Tuck barked and wagged his tail, almost tripping over his massive paws.

Miriam sighed. She walked up to Robyn, gently stroked his cheek and kissed him on it. "Count me in too, Hodekin. I shall join thy band of merry rogues to aid the poor of Nottingham."

Robyn blushed. He glanced at Amanda and mouthed *thank you* to her.

Amanda smiled just about the same time she felt a sudden jolt in her chest. This strange, yet persuasive feeling radiated up toward her neck and face. She glanced down and saw that her Babel was vibrating and glowing. Things started to turn blurry. Buildings, carts, tents, animals, Robyn, Miriam, and the others went fuzzy, formless, as if evaporating into the air. Only Melody, Professor Lucas, and her classmates remained solid, real. A sudden gust of wind caressed her, and Amanda felt her whole body spin and move. She heard a sound like a door sliding open and looked around. The Arch of Atlantis stood a few steps away from her.

Reaching for the Timekeepers' log in the bib of her overalls, Amanda pulled it out, unlatched the clasp and turned over the front cover to reveal the crystal trident. She carefully removed it and stuffed the log back down her bib. Amanda walked up to the closest column, stuck her foot into a crevice, and climbed up to place the trident in the keystone of the arch. A face suddenly appeared in the archway.

It was Lilith, and she was beaming.

19. *Mission Accomplished*

"Well done, Timekeepers," Lilith announced. "Time has remained unchanged. All is well, and everything is as it should be."

Amanda blew out a sigh of relief. *Good. Timekeepers—one. Belial—nothing.*

"What was Max Tarbush's creepy comeback all about, Lilith?" Jordan asked.

"Max Tarbush is what is called a Dreg, Jordan Jensen," Lilith explained.

Drake wrinkled his brow. "I can think of a better name for Tarbush. Scum-sucking bottom feeder comes to mind."

Lilith gave into a half-smile. "Your description is closer than you think, Drake Bailey. Dregs are people who have done nothing but give the worst part of themselves to the world while they were alive. Belial collects Dregs and sends them out to act on his behalf. But fear not, as Dregs can be easily identified by the black slime they ooze."

"So what was up with those ninja-style playing cards Tarbush used?" Ravi asked.

Lilith's face stiffened. This made her look grim. "Every Dreg possesses an evil device or ability, Ravi Sharma. Since Max

Tarbush was a corrupt gambler when he was living, he carries a cursed deck of cards for all eternity."

Amanda scratched her chin. Something bothered her. "But, Lilith, how do you expect us to fight against some douche-bag with an evil thingamajig or dark power?"

Lilith crinkled the corners of her eyes. "Real power comes from your intentions, Amanda Sault, and by using intention, integrity, and trust anything is possible." Then she smiled fully, releasing the tension held in her face a moment ago. "And knowing that Dregs abhor anything made of silver will help in some situations."

Treena gasped. "Robyn's silver arrow! That explains Tarbush's freaky allergic reaction!"

Lilith nodded. "Silver is one of the purest metals, Treena Mui. It has the ability to repel anything impure."

"Meeting Sir George was a bonus too," Amanda added. "Without him, we'd be stuck in time forever."

"Sir George is an El, Amanda Sault," Lilith said. "He is the extreme opposite of a Dreg in every way. Els are the *shining ones*, those who live by the sacred laws and serve others. They are compassionate beings who give the very best of themselves in life, and as each Dreg is different, the same goes for an El."

Treena grinned. "So an El is kind of like meeting our fairy godmother, or in this case, fairy godfather."

"Something like that, Treena Mui," Lilith replied.

"What about Marcus Crowley?" Professor Lucas asked. "There wasn't any black slime oozing from him."

The professor was still dressed in Sir Gavin's armor.

Lilith bent her head sadly. "Marcus Crowley is not a Dreg, Professor Lucas. He is something much worse—Belial's chosen *Initiate*. I am sorry to say that he is now an instrument of evil."

"Don't be sorry, Lilith," Drake said, gritting his teeth. "That loser's a rotten apple."

Jordan nudged Ravi. "Hey, now's a good time to ask Lilith about that new superpower you've acquired."

Professor Lucas perked up. "Super power? What super power?"

Ravi shrugged. "I...I don't really know how to explain it. My myoelectric hand...it...does things...things by itself."

"Not by itself, Ravi Sharma," Lilith corrected. "You evoke it through your thoughts."

"Evoke? Thoughts?" Drake said. "What's Lilith talking about, Ravi?"

Ravi stared at his right hand for a moment. His face twitched. "I...I think she means that if I'm in an intense situation, then whatever I'm thinking about in that moment triggers my hand to respond to help me solve the problem, like when I was trying to stop Jordan or figuring a way to reach Professor Lucas's hat."

Lilith smiled. "Well done, Ravi Sharma. As I have said, you have what you need with you, as well as—"

"—the *unseen power* inside me," Ravi finished for Lilith. He touched his hand and smiled. "Thanks for the crystal battery, Lilith, even if I can only use it during Timekeeper missions."

Lilith placed her hands together and bowed. "Thank you for trusting."

Amanda sighed, thinking what the future held for them. *Crowley. Belial. Dregs. Evil instruments.* It was so anti-Disneyland. She stuffed her hands in both pockets and felt a thick elastic band. She cringed, now knowing what it was, and pulled it out.

She tossed it at Jordan. "Hey, Jockstrap, thanks for the use of—"

"My jockstrap!" His face flashed to crimson as he quickly stuffed it into his backpack. Then he winced, shaking a finger. "Oww! Geez, Uncle John, one of the lures on your stupid fishing hat cut my—" Jordan stopped. He did a double take inside his backpack. "Hey, who put this knife in here?"

"Wil Scathlocke did," Lilith answered.

"Why would he do that?" Ravi asked.

"Wil Scathlocke finally found the justice and peace he was longing for and no longer needed to carry it," Lilith explained. "Both the dagger and Sir Gavin's armor are gifts from time. It is time's way of repaying all of you for what you have accomplished. After all, good deeds deserve good rewards."

"Well, they're wicked-awesome gifts, Lilith," Drake said, grinning. "But I still could have used a golden skateboard."

"Hey, wait a minute," Professor Lucas said strumming his fingers against the breastplate of his armor. "I know of a couple of antiquity dealers who would love to get their hands on these artifacts. They'd pay big bucks for sure."

Melody snapped her fingers. "That's a brilliant idea, John. Once you've acquired a buyer, we could use the money you receive to invest toward the children's future."

"Excellent! Like a college or university fund?" Professor Lucas probed.

Melody grinned and then winked at the professor. "Precisely, Sir Galahad."

Amanda felt her heart gush; it beat differently than it had before. Her entire body tingled. Everything seemed perfect in her life now, as if she was connected, plugged into something bigger and better than she could ever imagine. No one had considered her future before. Now it somehow looked brighter and clearer. Amanda hugged herself and smiled. Things were going to be different now. Much different.

"Before you go, there is something I wish to share," Lilith said, as she raised both her arms. "I was one of the First Timekeepers."

"Really?" Amanda dropped her jaw and released her arms at the same time. "How did you become a Timekeeper, Lilith?"

"That is a story for another time, Amanda Sault," she replied with a wink.

Then Lilith clapped her hands together seven times. The whirling rainbow instantly appeared and Amanda was gently drawn into it. Her last thought was that they were all going home—their Timekeeper journey was over, their mission complete.

The End

Acknowledgements

Life is a team effort. Period. Nothing is done without the help and support of others. The following people are in some way connected to the fabric of this work, to which I am eternally grateful:

Thank you to the staff at Mirror World Publishing; Justine Alley Dowsett, Murandy Damodred, and Robert Dowsett who invested in me and my time travel series, I really appreciate this fantastic opportunity and all your wonderful support and guidance. Special thanks to my cover artist Kelly Shorten, whose creative visualization gave my book a presence in this world.

Thank you to my family: my hubby Mike, my mother Peggy, my children Michelle, Jennifer, and Brandon. And to my brothers Gregg and Ian, who've given me lots of writer-fodder throughout our formative years.

Thank you to my prodders and teachers: Mrs. Jayne Greer, my seventh grade teacher, Jackie Hart, my BFF, Leslie Colwell, who got me into this mess in the first place, Tom Arnett, my first writing teacher, Barbara White and Sheila Nollert, my writing circle cohorts, Brian Henry, my writer workshop teacher, my first beta-reader Kelsey Bolt and my last beta-reader Kristian Gallant, and all the authors who I have connected with and have supported me in this amazing venture—you know who you are.

About the Author

Sharon Ledwith is the author of the middle-grade/young adult time travel series, THE LAST TIMEKEEPERS, and is represented by Walden House (Books & Stuff) for her teen psychic series, MYSTERIOUS TALES FROM FAIRY FALLS. When not writing, researching, or revising, she enjoys reading, exercising, anything arcane, and an occasional dram of scotch. Sharon lives a serene, yet busy life in a southern tourist region of Ontario, Canada, with her hubby, one spoiled yellow Labrador and a moody calico cat. Connect with her on her website: www.sharonledwith.com

To learn more about our authors and our current projects visit: www.mirrorworldpublishing.com or follow @MirrorWorldPub or like us at www.facebook.com/mirrorworldpublishing

We appreciate every like, tweet, facebook post and review and we love to hear from you. Please consider leaving us a review online or sending your thoughts and comments to info@mirrorworldpublishing.com

Thank you.

CPSIA information can be obtained at www.ICGtesting.com
Printed in the USA
LVOW11s0415230615

443433LV00002B/139/P